Touched

Acknowledgements

Many people encouraged me and offered invaluable responses to the manuscript during its lengthy gestation. In particular, I thank Betsy Warland for ongoing, multifaceted support; Jill Goodacre for spiritual midwifery as well as practical aid; and David Earle for artistic nurturance that rekindled hope.

Touched

Jodi Lundgren

Anvil Press Publishers • Vancouver

Touched
Copyright © 1999 by Jodi Lundgren

Anvil Press
Suite 204-A 175 East Broadway,
Vancouver, B.C. V5T 1W2 CANADA

All rights reserved. No part of this book may be reproduced by any means without the prior written permission of the publisher, with the exception of brief passages in reviews. Any request for photocopying or other reprographic copying of any part of this book must be directed in writing to the Canadian Copyright Licensing Agency (CANCOPY) One Yonge Street, Suite 1900, Toronto, Ontario, Canada, M5E 1E5.

This is a work of fiction. While some of the action takes place in identifiable settings, the characters are fictional.

Printed and bound in Canada
First Edition
Cover design: Leigh Lundgren
Cover illustration: Meg Walker

CANADIAN CATALOGUING IN PUBLICATION DATA

Lundgren, Jodi 1966–
Touched

ISBN 1-895636-25-6

1. Mental illness-Fiction   I. Title
PS8573.U542T68 1999   C813'.54   C99-911158-2
PR9199.3.L84T68 1999

Represented in Canada by the Literary Press Group
Distributed by General Distribution Services

The Canada Council | Le Conseil des Arts
for the Arts | du Canada

BRITISH
COLUMBIA
ARTS COUNCIL
We acknowledge the support of the Province of British Columbia
through the British Columbia Arts Council

Anvil Press gratefully acknowledges The Canada Council for the Arts and the B.C. Arts Council for their support of our publishing program.

for the hazelnut trees and their analogues

touched

(verb) To have put the hand, finger, or some other part of the body on or against something.

(adj.) 1) Affected with some feeling or emotion, moved or stirred.

    2) Not quite normal mentally; slightly crazed.

JADE

Family Names—Excerpts from the Notebook

Pregnant with me, my mother visited British Columbia and admired a mineral prized for its deep green colour. A hard, tough stone well-suited to be carved into intricate patterns. An official emblem of the province to which she hoped the family would move. Commonly called jade. Prized, I was the first daughter born to my parents. Who don't read dictionaries.

> jade (n): A broken-down, vicious, or worthless horse.
>
> A disreputable woman. A hussy (used contemptuously or playfully).
>
> (v.t.): to wear out by overwork or abuse.
>
> [<Spanish (*piedra de*) *ijada* (stone of) colic; pain in the side (because jade was thought to cure this) <Vulgar Latin *iliata*, *ilia*, flanks, groin.]

A broken-down old mare. Overworked, abused. A slut, a cocktease—they say playfully. Or with contempt. They like me, they despise me; I'm a flirt, I'm a whore. A pain in the side. And in the nether reaches of language, the darkest root, I'm ass, gash.

What of the jewel, semi-precious if not wholly so?
I'm worthless. I'm a cunt.

Jade, as a name? Diminutive of Judith? Praised, a Jewess (prized) . . . but close to Judas, betrayer of Christ? The vowel "u" is open, you can stab vertically into a "u," you can rape it. My high school French teacher taught us to put the circumflex on *août* over the "u" to keep the rain out.

Apparently God is protecting his little Judith by covering the vulnerable spot. Not "u" but "a." If you put a roof over the u in "cunt," u *cant* get into the space.

My surname brands me as my father's possession. His home is his castle, so he must be King. When I was a child, he called me Princess. I live on crown land, third in line to the throne.

My father's father was named Edgar: *rich*, *spear*. My father's name, Harold, means *army*, *power*. Those who carry the spear hold the power in this militaristic world: the phone book lists my father as "King Harold." Must I reject my heritage and change my name? What if my ancestors "held the spear" responsibly? But the very act of weapon-bearing intimidates and threatens. And how many patriarchs, encouraged to view their wives and daughters as belongings, don't assert "property rights"?

Maybe I can subvert the patronymic with a gerund. Not King but K-ing, an action, like skiing or hiking. Lineage in motion.

My father's mother, daughterless, bequeathed her opal ring to me. Her name, Louise, says: *hear*, *fight*. Her gem flickers like a torch.

My mother's name derives from my father's nickname, Harry—change the *y* to *i* and add *et*. Her name is the feminine complement but *not* the diminutive, *not* Harriette. As *home*, *rule*, (Harri)et both contains and exceeds the masculine. She maintains her own sphere of power.

«1»

—Tell me a story about the Prairies.
—You were born on the Prairies!
—I know, but I don't remember it. Tell me a story about snow.
—Snow. All right. I can remember one time it was snowing so hard and we had you kids with us, your mom was carrying you and I was pulling your two brothers behind me on a sleigh, we had just gone out for a walk, it was around Christmas time, but a blizzard come up so heavy we knew we'd never find our way home. When it surrounds you on all sides like that you lose your sense of direction. We happened to be right near a farmhouse so we made our way through the drifts, hoping that someone would be home and would let us in to wait out the storm. Of course there was no one there. We even tried the doors, thinking that we'd just let ourselves in, we didn't think they'd mind, I mean, we had you kids to think of, but it was shut up tight. So then Harriet said, what about the barn? Well fortunately it was open and so we went in there to wait out the storm among the pigs and the cows. We all curled up to conserve body heat, you know, and eventually we all fell asleep. You can imagine what the farmer felt when he came in to do the evening milking, and there was a whole family camped out in his barn.

JADE

Night: Twice I circle the waterfront lot next to Merlin's without seeing Yseult's white Toyota. She may have parked elsewhere—should I check the bar, or go home? Tail lights flash and an engine revs. In front of me, a jeep is vacating a spot under a streetlight. I take it.

Two steps from the car, I'm halted by the weight of my leather jacket—gift from my parents, it's too precious to entrust to the smoky darkness of a nightclub. I slip out of it and lay it across the back seat, where it sprawls, purple, the slit of the zipper parting to reveal the silky fuchsia lining.

Exposed to the night in a thin cotton blazer, I hug my chest. My bubble-gum pumps tap the asphalt as I aim for the door with the swirl of stars.

Someone is entering the bar just ahead of me: I know the proud carriage, the confident walk that affirms life with every step. "Hey, Duncan Nott!"

"Hey, hello, you," he responds, spinning with the quickness of a dog chasing its own tail, not wanting to be caught out.

"What are you doing here?"

"I was at a stag party and the guys conned me into giving them a ride. Designated driver, you know."

When I ask about my essay, his upper back stiffens and he amplifies his voice to a hollow boom. "Yes, I've marked the papers, but I'm not telling you your grade on a Friday night—not after midnight, anyways."

He walks on and, facing him, I side-step into the club. Half a semester's pent-up attraction fuels my chatter. I can't tell whether he's listening until finally he inclines his head like a tolerant parent, somewhat amused, and offers to buy me a drink.

At the bar, empty glasses hang upside down above our heads like microphones on a film set. Gem-coloured bottles of liqueur glint from their nooks as our conversation unfolds. I say our society forces people into moulds—dumb jock or geeky intellectual—whereas he's an iconoclast (thinking finally, my equal), and he says "Yeah, I could have been an Olympic squash player."

"No you couldn't have."

"Yes, I won the B.C. Open and—"

"Squash isn't an Olympic sport."

As he puzzles, I use my advantage to tack: "Every time a student says something in class, you act like it's nothing new to you, just something you've thought through before. You always have to be in control."

"Harold Bloom says—"

"I hate him!"

"You both love and hate him," Duncan insists. "Every emotion contains its opposite."

People jostle us as they squeeze past on their way to the dance floor. I place my lips close to Duncan's ear to be heard through the blaring rock music.

"Why did your parents name you after a hick town whose only claim to fame is a giant hockey stick?"

"I think they named me after where I was conceived."

"Duncan, B.C.?"

"No, the parking lot of Dunkin' Donuts."

His irreverence floors me, but I rally. "So then . . . 'Nott' refers to the donut hole. As in noughts-and-crosses."

"That's right, I'm the empty signified."

"Well, Zero, do you dance?"

"Dance? I like talking to you."

"You just don't want to be seen," I snap, meaning, *seen with me*. His features betray nothing. Only his eyes change: pupils huge in the dimness, they absorb my pique. Our legs have been digging into each other under the bar, but now I'm sliding off my stool and fumbling for my purse. He touches my elbow. "I like dancing to slow songs," he concedes.

"The DJ just announced that this was the last fast song, dummy, that's why I was asking you."

We edge onto the dance floor, where odours of sweat and spilled beer mix into air thick with cigarette smoke. He bends his head so that the bridges of our noses touch. The first time, stunned, I don't respond, but the second time he nuzzles me, I tilt up my chin for a liquid kiss.

"Listen to the lyrics," I cry when the slow song starts.

The singer promises to be my "father figure" if I put my "tiny hand" in his. "Father figure! I don't need another one."

My professor squeezes me and purrs, "Yeah, listen to the lyrics," as the singer croons that he wants to feel me "warm and naked."

Thrilled to be desired, I clasp my hands tighter around Duncan's neck and angle my groin into his. As we leave the dance floor, I look back and, catching his eyes on my ass, say, "Can I get a ride home with you?"

He nods.

I excuse myself to the washroom where I consult strange women. "I was just slow-dancing with one of my professors and he kissed me. He's marking one of my essays this weekend. What should I do?"

"Depends whether you want an 'A' on your paper," the first woman answers in a harsh voice.

"It's not like that—I'm attracted to him."

"Then go for it!"

The second woman I ask, who's gripping the counter and leaning into the mirror, stops teasing her moussed, straw-coloured hairdo and turns to me, still bent at the waist as though with stomach cramp. She bats vacant blue eyes. "I don't know what to say."

"I mean, you can't think about the wife, can you? That's his responsibility, isn't it?"

She shakes her head, clearly at a loss. I return to the bar where a fresh glass of wine and another beer have appeared.

Duncan's buddies have gathered to claim their rides home, and he kisses me in front of them. They ogle until he says, "Scram," and then, grinning, they wander off.

As we cross the parking lot, I critique Duncan's recent lecture on *King Lear* and filial ingratitude. "You made parenting out to be such a self-sacrificing activity, but it's not. I don't particularly admire parents; to most people, kids are just an extension of their own ego." I'm aware that he's a father: I risk near-insults with heady pleasure.

"But there are two types of people you can bring into the world, those who would push The Button and those who wouldn't."

"What Button?" I say, scorning this dangerous myth.

"Any button," he says. "I like talking to you. Can I do that?" He rubs my back.

"Sure." I worm my own arm under his mottled leather coat and encircle his waist—the warmth of his flesh radiates through his cotton shirt. We arrive at a ramp and pick our way between cross beams and wire mesh to the wharf, then we're alone among sleeping boats and restless waves. We neck, pressing our bodies together. He says, "We can either go to your place or get a hotel room downtown. As for my place . . . ."

We travel in Duncan's family-sized station wagon, leaving my car downtown for the night. I insist that we take Dallas Road and follow the curves of the shoreline home. Across the street from my house, we lean against the car. "I can't sleep with you, it's not safe."

He pulls open his jacket like someone selling hot watches on a street corner. "I gave Brian some of these at the stag tonight—French safes."

I still hesitate and he says, "Another time, maybe."

"Oh, no, I want you to come in."

"I'd definitely like to see more of you."

"Wait here while I go in and check things out. Then when I flash my light on and off, you come—"

"Right then?"

"And I'll ope' the casement."

Inside, I kick off my shoes. In the kitchen, I grab a plastic tumbler and fill it with wine from the keg in the fridge. Then I go to my room and lock the door. I peel off my grey skirt and my pink nylons as if preparing for sleep. When I let Duncan in the window, his eyes lock on my French-cut briefs. He stands by my desk with his hands in his pockets and keeps staring while I sink to the bed. At last his gaze embarrasses me and I reach for a blanket to cover myself. That's when he pushes me onto my back.

When I close my eyes I forget who I'm with and opening them surprises me. Our clothes come off. "You have lovely skin, you're so—"

"Smooth and sleek," I suggest.

"Smooth and sleek," he agrees as he strokes me. "There's just something about your presence—"

"My absence."

"That's right, there's something about your absence . . . you are Desire, aren't you, as Woman?"

"Perpetually deferred."

"Well, screw delayed gratification, I say."

I suck in my breath as he touches my clitoris. Encouraged, he plunges his finger inside me and slides it back and forth. "Should I get one of those things?" he says.

"I don't know, I've never done this before."

"Me neither, not before tonight! Shall we?"

"I don't know, I don't know. I don't— No."

He flips me onto my stomach. "Second best thing," he murmurs.

"What are you doing?"

"Just hold still." The bedsprings jounce as he manoeuvres himself crosswise on top of me. I feel claustrophobic as in the children's game of dogpile. His penis digs into my side, finds a hollow in between ribcage and hip and then chafes, fast, faster . . .

"An ellipsis in poetry is always an orgasm," he said earlier. "Always."

I shift out of the wet spot in the mattress. Duncan dresses with brisk movements as though trying to erase the memory of a doctor's cold instruments against his skin. His fingers fly over his buttons—it's four a.m. by my bedside clock. I pull on my fuzzy pajamas with the snowflake pattern, the ones my mom gave me for Christmas. When he stands to leave, I make him pick me up for a good-bye kiss. As I open the window to let him out, I knock my wine cup into a stuttering roll. I can almost hear the uneasy shifting of bodies in my parents' room.

HAROLD

B*irth*: Harold sprang out the hospital doors. A pink-skied dawn was tingeing the air with hints of apples in the cellar, maple leaves on the ground, bales of hay stacked in the barn. Harvest. Harriet had been in labour all night and had finally given birth as the moon was setting. It was six-thirty by his wrist watch. If he left now, he could make it back to Flatbush in time to start work. But arrangements had been made: the boys were at a sitter's; a sign posted in the office window said, "Gone to Edmonton to Have a Baby! Back Oct.10." And October ninth was just beginning.

Edmonton felt like home—it was where he'd attended university and worked as a junior accountant. Opening his own firm five years ago had meant moving north—but it had been well worth it. He'd been brought up by an entrepreneur, and if the service station wasn't exactly a thriving operation, Dad had sure been right about the value of being your own boss. He could take the day off without answering to anyone.

Wide awake from the vending machine coffee he'd drunk through the night from plastic cups, refreshed by the morning air, Harold decided to drive home. Not home to Flatbush, home to Olds, to tell his folks the news in person.

Just beating rush hour, he negotiated the familiar grid of streets and was soon headed for Calgary, feeling released, like a student going home for Thanksgiving. The highway was flanked by fields of yellow stubble. The prairie sky opened wide above the open road.

As he travelled south, the landscape developed bumps and shadows. The caffeine wore off and his stomach rumbled. He'd have some scrambled eggs and a fresh cup of coffee at Mom's—maybe she'd have some of her rice pudding in the fridge. There was the sign: Olds Exit 1 mile.

As he passed the outlying farms and entered town, the reservoir tower loomed up like a hut on stilts, menacing him with the memory of his high school graduation night. He shuddered as he continued on to his parents' house, a stucco bungalow they'd moved into after he and his brothers left home.

He leapt to the side door, knocked, and burst in without waiting. "Anybody home?"

"In here."

Breakfast dishes were piled in the sink. A pair of houseflies was orbiting an open jar of jam—raspberry, the seedy kind that gave Harold a stomach ache. He crossed the kitchen to the living room. Sunbeams slanted from windows at his back into a sea of dust motes, slowly twirling. On a couch in the far corner of the room, Harold's mother sat with her feet tucked up, cigarette in hand, a magazine spread in her lap. Behind her, velvet curtains were drawn against the morning. An inner room harboured her piano, its keyboard shut.

"It's a girl!"

"Where's Harriet?"

"She's in the hospital. The baby just came at dawn, and I decided to drive down and tell you in person."

Harold approached his mother. Besides the couch, stacked with magazines, the only places to sit either didn't face her or weren't close enough for easy conversing, so he halted on the rug in front of her. Hands clasped behind his back, he dug his toe under the tassels and cleared his throat. His mother sipped from a crystal glass.

"Harriet's lucky. I always wanted a girl. But I got three boys. What are you going to call her?" Harold's mother took a breath between each sentence.

"We haven't talked about it yet. But we'll give her your name as a middle name, of course. Louise."

She sucked on her cigarette. "Why do that? It's an ugly name. Old-fashioned. Why not call her Ginger? Or—" She was cut short by a coughing fit.

He longed to escape from the wracking sounds, but he braced himself and weathered them. As soon as they subsided, he said, "You know, I'm starving. Do you mind if I have something to eat?"

"Help yourself. There's jam there."

Harold was scraping butter across his toast when his name was whispered. "Mother! You startled me." Surely she had shrunk. Even in her prime she had been under five feet, but now she bent over a cane, gnome-like.

"Harold. Give this to the baby."

She held something between thumb and index finger: a ring, its milky stone bracketed by gold filigree.

"Mom, are you sure?"

"It's an opal. It's her birthstone, and mine. If anyone else were to wear it, they'd be cursed. See how it flickers in the light? You give it to her. She'll shimmer like that."

"Thanks, Mother." Harold gripped his plate of toast in both hands and dropped into a chair. There was a knot the size of a prune in the centre of his chest and it was starting to swell. He held his breath and willed it to shrivel. Otherwise, he would be split, like the opal by light, into a spectrum of emotions. The rainbow glints dulled to a uniform pearl when his mother set down the ring. Deprived of light, the iridescence faded until the stone had almost no colour at all.

"I'll be off then," he called into the living room as soon as he'd eaten.

"You'd better. Think how Harriet must feel. Crazy running off like that."

"I guess I'll just stop by the garage with a box of cigars, tell Dad and Ernie."

"I'm sure they've got nothing better to do than stand around smoking, the way business is."

"It was good to see you."

"Have you got the ring?"

"Yes, Mother." In fact he hadn't. It was sitting on

the breakfast table, in the shadow of the jam jar, where she had placed it. He wondered what to put it in. The spice rack was full of little jars—there was an empty one. Allspice. He put the ring inside the jar and tucked the jar into his coat pocket.

"Watch out for your daughter."

He latched the screen door behind him, then filled his lungs with clean air. *His daughter.* He liked the sound of that. Girls were more your own than boys. And he *would* protect her.

The gravel shoulder crunched under the Buick's wheels as Harold pulled onto the road. He forbade himself to look at the house. She never waved. A stab of hope forced him to turn his head. His glance sailed like a rope thrown uphill to a climbing partner. It slapped the wall of living room drapes and snaked to the ground.

JADE

Saturday: In the morning I buy grapefruit juice at the corner store to drink on the beach. My stomach has shrunk into a fist and refuses food. The inside of my head feels dry and hot, as though it's under a sun lamp. I lean back against a log and shut my eyes. The surf sloshes forward, drags back. I give in to the rhythm.

At night my parents attend the opera so I pilfer the sherry and call Duncan at his office (he's working late Saturday night).

"I'd like to be outdoors with you," he says. We descend beach stairs, mount a gutter outlet, and survey the sea as from the prow of a ship. He embraces me from behind. "Where are you going in a relationship like this?"

Does he mean "you" generally or specifically? I shrug for both. "I was involved with a married man before."

"What was it like?"

I shrug again. "It wasn't right."

As we climb the weathered steps, he hooks one Levi's belt loop with a finger and spins me around for a kiss. "I think we should do it," I say.

"What? It, the ambiguous referent."

"Sex!" Arms crossed, chin jerking, I almost stamp my foot.

Instead I unfold my arms and stroke his crotch. The vine-covered banks on either side of the staircase exude the mustiness of winter sleep. He slips a hand inside my jacket and through the armhole of my tank top to clamp my breast. "Shall we go to my office, then?" He breathes low.

As we reach the top of the staircase, a beam of light sweeps the lawn. Duncan and I freeze in the shadow of a tree. "I think that's my dad with the flashlight. We must have let the cat out."

"Let's just keep walking." A vacant lot divides us from my father. We head for the road.

"Are we going to your office?"

"No, I don't think so. Seeing your dad there really did something to the old hormones."

"I know what you mean."

"No, I mean, it made me realize something about you."

"What? You think I'm a kid." Indignant. "Come on, I can't go in there and face them right now, let me just come along and keep you company for awhile. Please?"

Gritty English Department carpet scuffs my knees. We've struggled awkwardly out of our clothes, my jeans too tight around the calf, the dilemma posed by his socks disconcerting us both.

Gloom chills the office. The uncurtained window gapes black. Books sag against each other and display their spines with reluctance. Duncan kneels stiffly a few feet from me. His penis has filled with blood and risen with no apology. I fall forward onto my hands, take its mushroom tip in my mouth. He lets me suck for just seconds before he raises me by the shoulders and we tumble to the floor. He rests his weight on his elbows and looks down on me without kissing me, says, "I like to watch." In tandem, my palms trace a path on his body, rise over the hump of his buttocks, curve around his waist, push up his smooth chest, encircle the trunks of his arms. When I stretch my arms above my head, he draws my wrists together in his hand.

"I don't understand it. I see you lying under me, so beautiful, but . . . I don't . . . too many commercials, I guess." He tries to write it off to our lack of birth control, but when he moves his head, campus lights play over his face and reveal his puzzlement.

"It's easy for you," I exclaim.

"Oh, is it?"

"You've got a sex life."

"No, I'd love to be inside you right now," he insists. "And I want you around me, too."

"Mm—yeah." Equal partners.

But as he pulls away, I cry, "*When?*" It's dangerous to release all those hormones and not climax. For the second night running, I'm anesthetized by alcohol and unrelieved lust. I dress with numb thrusts of my limbs and, at Duncan's insistence, leave by myself. I drift from the building and melt into the softness of an early spring night, praying aloud: "I know you're there. I feel you around me. I've been listening to my instincts and trusting coincidence and that has led me here. I know this encounter happened for a reason."

Sensing someone, I turn my head. "Is that you?" I call. Duncan has heard me talking to "myself"; he says carefully, "I just wondered if you remembered where we were parked?" I've been walking in the "wrong" direction, far away, beginning the mystic plunge as I listen to all the voices. But it's not a Sylvia Plath suicide dive, it's discovering patterns in the world, patterns that were already encoded in the language.

When he drops me off, he says, "I think I'll sleep reasonably well tonight."

"A hell of a lot better than last night." After he left my room, I listened incessantly to R.E.M. on my headphones and didn't sleep at all. His glance darts to my face at this admission.

"It's given me something to think about, anyways," he says.

"I'll see you on Tuesday. Don't worry, I'll act *very* normal." I kiss him, but his lips don't yield, his face is boarded up against me.

As I open the front door of the house, my mother flies down the stairs in her nightgown. She approaches me with outstretched hands and searching eyes. "Are you all right?" Her face looks peeled without its layer of make-up. Her high-necked, long-sleeved flannel nightdress is edged at collar and cuffs with lace. The hem touches the floor and her stockinged feet peep out from underneath. "Where have you been? What happened?"

The doormat is my island in a sea of cold, pale tile. I shift my feet in suede ankle boots, bury my hands in the pockets of my leather coat. "Nothing, Mom."

"We came home and the back door was wide open. The stereo and all the lights were on. It looked just like someone had broken in the front door and you'd run out the back."

"I went for a walk on the beach."

"You've been out walking all this time? By yourself?"

I inspect my brown shag liferaft.

"Obviously you weren't by yourself," she says, half-accusingly. She draws back a little. "Your dad said I shouldn't worry." As her jaw begins to relax, the corners of her mouth turn down. "Are you really okay?"

"Yes, Mom, I'm fine. I'm sorry for leaving the door open."

My mother hitches up her gown to keep from tripping on her way back upstairs. I kick off my boots and leave them stranded on the doormat.

LOUISE

At fifteen, Louise played piano for the silent films in Olds. Musical scores arrived a day or two in advance of the reels; she learned what she could and sight-read the rest. The young people would crowd her in the street, and when she said she didn't know what the next film was about, they thought she was being mysterious. Louise had never received more than a few music lessons, most of them paid for with her own earnings. She practised on the church piano. Yet it was she, and not one of the girls whose parents had them learn music as a social grace, who had won the position of cinema pianist. As she played, she constantly flicked her eyes to the screen—galloping horses, speeding trains, men who walked like penguins all found their way through her fingers to the keys. Boys jockeyed to see her home after the show. She hummed whenever she walked.

One evening her escort grasped her elbow just before they reached her gate. Her back brushed the laurel border. One waxy leaf scratched her cheek. Behind the boy's shoulder loomed the neighbours' house, windows lit.

"May I kiss you?"

The boy's freckles didn't show up in the dusk; in fact, he looked nearly black and white, like a film star. Louise clutched the score to her chest. The boy's face moved closer. The parted lips, the drooping eyelids at first repulsed her and she recoiled. Then a lock of hair fell over his forehead and endeared him to her. Their lips met: yellow light and water so clear, it tasted sweet.

A roar and he was torn from her. "Get into the house. Now!"

Her father shoved her with the heel of his hand. "As for you—"

She heard scuffling in the gravel; the boy pleading "Sir—"; her father's voice muttering threats. A blow, then the soles of the boy's shoes hurrying away. She wasn't quick enough—her father found her behind the hedge. He struck her across cheek and mouth. Her face numbed, then burned. "No daughter of mine is going to be the talk of the town! That's the last time you play for the pictures."

She bent to pick up the score he had knocked from her arms, and he kicked it away.

« 2 »

—So this is the Bow River?
—That's right. Not to be confused with the other river that crosses Calgary—the Elbow.
—You're joking.
—That's the absolute truth. You know, when your Granny and Granddad got married, they drove to Banff for their honeymoon. They packed a picnic lunch and they stopped to eat it here, beside the Bow. My mother wanted to wash her hands before she ate—they didn't have Wet-Ones in those days, she had to use the river. Well, she didn't like to stick her hand in the water with her new ring on, so she took it off. Now, at that time, cars had running boards on the sides that went along under the door, to give you a place to step when you got into the car. There wasn't any other place handy, so she set her ring down on the running board, washed her hands and had lunch. When the time came to leave, she didn't miss the ring; she'd hardly got used to wearing it yet. They drove almost all the way to Banff before she remembered what she'd done. She yelled out, "Stop the car!" She was shaking all over. They'd been driving for miles on a bumpy gravel road and she was sure the ring had long since bounced into the ditch. They pulled off to the side of the road, she opened her door—and the ring was still there! Sitting right there where she left it after all those miles.

JADE

Weekdays: In dance class the teacher, Aristotle, calls, "Jade—be a bird." I test my still-wet wings, slowly flapping them up and down until they dry and I gain confidence in my ability to fly. I rise onto my toes, feet in fifth, and bourré on the spot with the frenetic energy of a hummingbird. Then I take off in flight, leaping in grand jetés across the room. The whole flock follows my lead and we swoop like starlings trying to choose a tree to land in, swayed by a communal will, which emanates, for the moment, from me, or through me.

In another exercise, we pair up and stand side by side. Slowly one person leans into her partner, contours fitting into contours, so that she bends, too. Eventually, the leaner reaches the point where she would lose her balance and fall without the support of the other, and so she must let go of her instinct for self-preservation, and trust. She can trust her partner not to hurt her because she knows that she doesn't want to hurt her partner. Conventional physical boundaries corrode as it ceases to matter where one body ends and the other begins. The dancers play off the centrifugal force. Limits vanish.

We retreat to the inner studio for linked-body stretches. Warm wooden walls draw close in the dim light as African drums faintly menace. A dozen or more dancers, mostly lithe teenagers, grip each other's thighs, cradle backs, grind pelvises into the floor. Aristotle manipulates the hips of a pubescent boy. Someone rises to leave, arm bent across her belly, hand supporting her head. Aristotle talks to her in a low voice, resting his broad palm on her shoulder, but she insists on leaving. Afterwards, he turns to the rest of us and explains, "She was nauseous. It's very natural to have to throw up when you're doing this; I encourage people to just go to the bathroom and then come back. We're stirring up rhythms and feelings that go deep into your gut. We might be unlocking some doors in your body that you have kept sealed off for years, even from yourself."

After class we form a crescent on the floor and Aristotle explains that we've been experimenting with vulnerability. When we break through the shell of defences, we discover the self that is the source of expression. A girl behind me says she feels like hugging everyone.

"So that's the meaning of life, then!" I exclaim. "We all have something to say!"

A few people glance my way uncertainly but Aristotle confirms my zeal with a smile. "That's what I think it is."

At school, Duncan communicates with me while lecturing on Donne. " 'The Canonization' is the impassioned declaration of a man approaching middle age—note his 'five grey hairs.' He demands that he and his lover be permitted to consummate their passion. There is a strong sense of societal opposition, yet the speaker insists that their love will injure no one. In fact, with typical audacity, Donne indicates that he and his lover, through their carnal relationship, will be canonized and provide a pattern for all the world. Donne knows that not only must physical passion be yielded to—but that it is the path to ideal love." Duncan punctuates this last sentence of the lecture by propelling himself backwards from the lectern with his chest (hands in pockets) and sliding along the adjacent table, leaning forward, until he's level with me. Our eyes meet and our faces mirror each other with a smile broad enough to enlighten the whole campus.

On Thursday, when Duncan has office hours, I venture to see him around quarter to twelve. Another student has claimed him, so I squat on my heels in the hallway. I hear her laugh and say something about herself—they're not discussing literature, she's flirting with him. I deny myself jealousy: I have a theory about human relationships that would eliminate jealousy, I just want the chance to convey it. I hear him say, "Is there anyone else waiting to talk to me?" When she says, with a throaty chuckle, "They're just pounding down your door," I rise and mutter, "Forget it." I run out of the building, almost knocking down a frail-looking, white-haired prof as I round a corner.

I want to escape, but I'm carless. I crouch in the lee of a cedar sapling, tears welling up, until I remember that the bar in the SUB opens at noon. I toss back two glasses of watered-down white wine, glancing at the just-printed student newspaper. In the classifieds, I notice an ad:

> Are you seeking a reliable connection to Duncan? Ride with me! Prefer articulate female, early twenties, who likes the Renaissance. Share gas, donuts & conversation.

This is not a carpool ad, it's a love note from Professor Nott. Under the surface of *"commute to Duncan"* lies a message directed at me: *"commune with Duncan."* I respond to the injunction by returning to Clearihue and pressing the elevator button. When the door slides back, he's not inside. I'll ride with him another time.

On the third floor, Duncan stands in his doorway talking to Nina, my feminist theory professor. When he sees me, he lifts his eyebrows and points to his office. I hold his gaze. "Yes, I'm coming to see you." Nina witnesses our meeting, then takes her leave.

It's the first time Duncan and I have spoken since I kissed him goodbye, but this won't be a selfish conversation: in the personal are crystallized concerns of epic scope. "I have something to say." He invites me to sit in his old, overstuffed armchair. "You've been lecturing that the way to ideal love is through physical love, when ideal love is unattainable. If people could give up the attempt to possess the ideal, their relationships could persist and grow instead of collapsing."

A knock on the door. Duncan says, "Come in." A secretary enters and checks an item of business with him. As the secretary leaves, a student arrives to collect an essay. She neglects to shut the door behind her, and for a moment I long for private time with Duncan. But I am mindful of my mission. "The myth that we can achieve self-completion in another person has been incredibly damaging. As a society we are enslaved to the myth of romantic love."

"But you aren't." Duncan swivels to face me, eyes gleaming.

Is he mocking me? No, smiling in admiration. "I've had my eyes opened," I say, looking into his. "We need to break the association between sex and ownership. Marriage is obsolete."

"Haven't sex and marriage *always* been antithetical?"

"Of course. Familiarity kills desire."

"Like curiosity and the cat?"

"It's no joke. I think we should abolish possessive pronouns when they refer to people: *my* wife, *my* boyfriend. We need to loosen our jealous grip on each other."

"You and I?"

"No, people in general."

"Because I was going to say . . . "

"We need to split open the dyad at the heart of the nuclear family."

"Sounds like an atom bomb."

"It could have that much impact. We have to realize that genital sex is only one possible expression of sexuality: the potential is infinite. The fact is that *all* encounters are sexed. When you accept this, the whole concept of adultery becomes absurd. Possessiveness towards your lover disappears when you realize that everyone you meet is, on some level, a sexual partner. I'm coining the term *infisexuality*."

"*Infisexual*—I like that. So you're saying that there is no valid distinction between the kind of sensory exchange you and I are having right now—I'm hearing your words, I'm seeing you, on a subconscious level I'm probably smelling you as well—and sexual intercourse?"

"Right. I think sexuality is a continuum, and the distinctions we make between its different forms are arbitrary."

After a time, I glide satisfied into the hallway and let destiny hook and pull me where it will.

« 3 »

—Granddad owned a gas station and sold cars. Does that mean he was rich?

—Well, it was the Depression, you know, so people didn't have any money. He gave a lot of credit, or sometimes a farmer would come in with a sack of grain or a pig, and he'd accept it as barter for a tank of gas or a new tire. My mother was awful hard on him for that.

"What am I going to do with a pig?" she'd say. But Dad felt in hard times people had to help each other out. And he was sure well-loved—he was voted in as mayor two times. People wanted him to run for Legislature but he never would—he didn't feel he was qualified because he only had a grade eight education.

—Really? You think he might have been elected?

—Oh he would have been elected. That's how popular he was.

HAROLD

"I don't know why we run a business at all, you just give away all your services."

Harold set his soup spoon on the saucer and rummaged through the pocket of his cardigan. He pulled out three or four balled up pieces of Kleenex and spread them on his knee. He inspected them, selected one and replaced the rest. Sheathed in tissue, his index finger twisted into his nostril. He raised his eyebrows to keep from blinking and let his corneas glaze.

"I don't know why it's so important to you to be a notary public. It was one thing to do it in Flatbush, but it doesn't make any sense in the city. We'd be far better off if you spent your time cultivating new clients. Especially with H&R Block moving in across the street. I don't know how you expect us to survive."

"Why can't you just charge for the notary public services?"

Jade's question was directed to Harold, but Harriet replied. "That's a darn good question, Jade. I'd like to know the answer to that myself."

"Jade, your mother and I are talking."

"You always have to be the selfless public servant. It would be fine if the business were healthier, but we're losing clients every year. You can't afford to be donating your time just so you can feel important. You think lawyers don't charge an arm and a leg for doing what you do? Anyway, you're an accountant! You should have jumped when that credit union wanted to bring you in-house, you'll never get an offer like that again, but would you? Oh no, you wouldn't go to work for anybody else because you were afraid of disappointing your father. Well, it won't do you much good to be 'self-employed' when it comes time to declare bankruptcy."

Harold poked the Kleenex back into his pocket and frowned at the table, shoulders slumped. He would never rage although Harriet's nagging wore him down like rain.

After lunch he watched Sunday football. Jade snuggled beside him and he tucked her against his ribs. She looked sweet in her pink pleated skirt and knee-socks. Her fair hair caught in barrettes. He dug out a roll of Lifesavers and popped a mint with his thumbnail to offer her.

Players ran, slammed each other and were wrestled to the ground. Every so often the camera zoomed in on one: arms akimbo, pacing on long, lean legs.

Harold held his breath until the whistle blew and then roared to life. "Yahoo!" He made fists and bounced on the chesterfield. He jumped to his feet and punched the air. If he kept his eyes fixed on the screen, the game was all that existed.

JADE

Barefoot Waonderings: On Saturday morning, I caper on a log in the brilliant February sunshine, blood speeding through my veins. The sun dances on the surface of Cadboro Bay, and people in wetsuits are braving the water with windsurfers. I smile at them and continue on my way to the University.

In the library I closet myself in a carrel to write in my Notebook.

> Anthropologists have found that alliances between kinship groups depend on the exchange of women. Used goods have little commodity value, so female relatives are off limits when it comes to sex.
> → Economics creates a universal taboo against incest.
>
> But to forbid incites desire—look at Eve and the Tree of Knowledge. So no wonder Freud finds incestuous *desire* universal (the Oedipal complex). Only he attributes it to *children*: every child unconsciously wants to be "seduced" by the parent of the opposite sex.

The smell of ageing books plugs my nostrils. The

drone of fluorescent lights engulfs me. I burst from the carrel and rush down the stairs, out of the library. In the empty courtyard, open space reassures me. Fresh air revives me.

I stretch out on a bench, face-down, and prop myself up to write:

> I am neither a virgin nor a whore: "I slept with a guy for fourteen months without sleeping with him" → refusing to let a colloquial expression dictate my behaviour. We were perpetuating stereotypes, we hadn't reached the point of liberation. I couldn't accept society's terms—I didn't want to be "deflowered," "penetrated." I needed to create my own word—infisexual—before "sleeping" with anybody.

I rise and rub my elbows where the ribbed stitch of my cotton sweater has dug grooves into my skin. The thought of peppermint tea propels me to the cafeteria, where I find Yseult dipping carrot sticks in yoghurt-dill dressing. Her high ponytail flops over one ear.

"Yseult! I'm working on something that could save the world from nuclear war." I show her the page where I've scrawled: "WE ARE ALL ACTORS & ENTERTAINERS, COMEDIANS, DANCERS, SINGERS, SCREAMERS, LOVING, INFI-SEXUAL BEINGS!"

"What's 'infi-sexual'?"

"It's my vision for the future of sexuality. Sexuality is expressed in an infinite number of ways. It can't be fixed, can't be chained to the service of some ideal like marital monogamy."

"And what does that have to do with nuclear war?"

"You know The Button that everyone talks about? That can be reconceived as the collective clitoris. Instead of mass annihilation, we'll have mass orgasm."

"As in, the world ends with a bang?"

"No, no, the world won't end, it will be redeemed. In Christian mythology, the Fall was collective. So it's only logical that the Second Coming will be collective, too."

Yseult ziplocks her remaining carrots. "I don't think this affair with Duncan is doing you any good."

"Marriage is an institution but you can't say that we've transgressed the arbitrary laws because he hasn't put his penis inside me, therefore he hasn't been unfaithful to his wife. We're also inside the institution of the University and breaching behavioural codes for professors and students, and yet not, for the same reason."

"I don't give a shit about the moral point of view, Jade. I'm just worried that you're getting in over your head." She checks her watch. "It's time for aerobics. Are you coming?"

"I'll meet you there." Getting in over my head? Going over *her* head, more likely.

At home, my family eats dinner with the blinds up while a couple strolls on the vacant lot next door. They stand on the corner and stare in at us. The woman's dark eyes glow with a warm, perhaps adulatory, look. They've come to get me! I run into my room—she's still watching me—I yank down my blind.

Where have I seen those eyes before? "Come join our group," she's saying. I say, "No. No. I can't have a nervous breakdown, I can't lose this, this is too good to lose."

I pull out my Notebook:

"Every emotion contains its opposite."
YES, Duncan, and every NOtion contains its opposite.

NOTT

Naught	Knot
Absence	Presence
Nothing	All

All-or-nothing binary thinking is resolved in Duncan's name! (K)not. Zero is only ever an arbitrary designation: (w)hole. I am neither one thing nor another. No one is either one thing or another. CHRIST and ANTI-CHRIST is the ultimate in oppressive binary oppositions.
We don't need binary oppositions in order to think!

Love me, love me not.
Love me. Love me, Nott.
Dun*can*, Dun*can Nott*! *DUN* cannot love! But blonde can!
I am blonde! Duncan needs me to teach him how to love.

The night draws on. We've been taught to equate consciousness with pain and to escape from it for eight hours every night with the lights off—but when are crimes perpetrated? We need to stay awake, and keep an eye on each other.

My father, still dressed, pries open my door without knocking. He clutches the handle, looking from my desk to the floor and back again. "Shouldn't you be getting to bed?" His eyebrows slope towards each other, deepening the wrinkles across his forehead.

"No, I want to write."

"But you need to get some sleep."

"Didn't you just say a few days ago, nobody ever died from lack of sleep?" He can't deny that he did; we laughed at the dinner table about people who go into Emergency at 3 a.m. for sleeping pills.

"Hey!" He lets go of the door knob and approaches my desk to pick up the miniature vodka bottle at my elbow. "Did you drink this whole thing?"

The wooden legs of my desk chair scrape against the tile floor as I pull back. "It's a tiny bottle. I needed it to relax."

"What else did you have?"

"Nothing. You're right to be distrustful, drugs are bad, but in a few days I won't need it any more. I just need to keep writing."

He tsks. For a few seconds he hovers in front of me, motionless. Mouth open, he exhales a puff of breath, stale like the air from inside a bicycle pump. I jerk my chair even further back, hitting the bookshelf behind me. My arms bristle with goose bumps. He bends to realign my waste bin with the edge of my desk, then straightens and shuffles towards the door. In the middle of the room he turns to face me again, arms folded, the empty bottle in one fist. His right knee jiggles as if to a jazz beat only he can hear. "Why don't you at least lie down and see if you can fall asleep? It's late."

"Okay, I'll try." He doesn't move. "I promise." He shuffles out of my room. He starts to shut the door but halts when it's the width of his face from the jamb. In this way, he frames his final stare. After his exit, bottles clink and thud in the kitchen as they're lifted out of the cupboard and then replaced, one by one.

I turn off my overhead light and move to the bed, switching on my bedside lamp. I prop my pillow under my stomach and continue to write. [Notebook entry]:

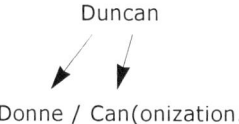

Donne / Can(onization.

Duncan and I are Donne's contemporary counterparts. When we conjoin, we will be "canonized for love"!

Every so often I collapse over my Notebook for fifteen minute catnaps with the light on.

The next day my mother says, "Jade, you're scaring me. You can't tell people things. They don't want to listen to you. You can't change the world."

"Who told you that?"

"Don't keep firing questions at me."

"I do have something unique to say. I can teach, not by telling people things they don't know, but by helping them to uncover things they know instinctively. Instincts are in the body; the body knows."

"That's obvious, Jade, you're not saying anything new." Her eyes spill over with fear and denial.

"What are you scared of?"

"You've turned into this gaunt, hollow-eyed creature. I don't recognize you. I just want you to be the old Jade."

"Well, I can't go back."

Back, back, the muscles of my neck and upper back ache with tension. I massage my own knots. I pour myself a glass of wine, then another.

"Hey! What are you doing? How much of that are you having?" My dad starts up from the couch in the TV room.

"I need to relax."

"That's not going to help you."

"You don't know how sore my back is, Dad."

"What did you do to it?" He scowls. "It's that aerobics you go to. You know there are physiotherapists now that specialize entirely in aerobics-related injuries?"

"I won't have any more." When I leave the kitchen I hear my mother's strained whine counterpointed by my father's bass interjections. Their voices chase each other in a fugue, a theme and variations with always another reprise. The composition gradually crescendos until it culminates in a heavy chord.

Accord. The word "doctor."

DIAGNOSTIC AND STATISTICAL MANUAL OF MENTAL DISORDERS

DSM-IV

Manic Episode

Episode Features

...The elevated mood of a Manic Episode may be described as euphoric, unusually good, cheerful, or high. Although the person's mood may initially have an infectious quality for the uninvolved observer, it is recognized as excessive by those who know the person well. The expansive quality of the mood is characterized by unceasing and indiscriminate enthusiasm for interpersonal, sexual, or occupational interactions.

Inflated self-esteem is typically present, ranging from uncritical self-confidence to marked grandiosity, and may reach delusional proportions. ... Despite lack of any particular experience or talent, the individual may embark on writing a novel... .

Frequently there is flight of ideas evidenced by a nearly continuous flow of accelerated speech... . Speech is sometimes characterized by joking, punning and amusing irrelevancies. ... Sounds rather than meaningful conceptual relationships may govern word choice.

Reprinted with permission from the Diagnostic and Statistical Manual of Mental Disorders, *Fourth Edition. Copyright 1994 American Psychiatric Association.*

JADE

It's Monday, Leap Day, and I want to point out to my Latin class that you can see the Olympic Mountains from the window of the Classics Department Library: Olympus, home of the Greek deities. *Heaven is a place on earth.*

I decide, however, that I need to spend the day with my mother, to reassure her. We walk along the damp sand at the beach, low-tide. The grey sky mirrors the sea and hints at rain.

She pressures me until I agree to see a doctor, for her sake. When we mount the beach stairs at the end of our walk, a nondescript beige sedan is driving up the hill out of our cul-de-sac, headlights on. I know it contains spies who have "checked out" the house in our absence, so I wave.

"Do you know them?"

"No, I didn't have to. All these cars are driving around with their lights on these days: the Spirit is in the machine. We don't have to be afraid of the machine."

And thus we don't have to be afraid of The Button

because what they don't want you to find out is that The Button is the Cosmic Clitoris and if we all Fell at once, we can all Come at once—redemption, the Multiple Coming. God said after the Great Flood that he would never kill his creatures again. Nuclear annihilation is not going to happen. Peace is unfolding even as we speak.

Dad comes home from work early; he has courses to attend.

"Jade, we're going to the doctor."

"Do you want to shut me up, Dad?"

"No, I don't want to shut you up."

"Let's go to the University then." Latin: *universi* = all together. "You have your lecture in the history of jazz and after that your continuing education seminar in accounting. Dad, you don't like drugs.

"Dad, what will they do to me if you take me to the doctor? They'll give me drugs and shut me up, Dad, didn't you just say you didn't want to shut me up?" *You can't argue with me, Dad, I don't want you to argue with me.*

I grab the door. "You can't own me, Dad."

"Jade."

I'm out the door.

"JADE!"

I run out of the house in my socks carrying shoes stained with blister blood, throw them onto the junk pile in my neighbour's yard, peel off my socks and toss them after. I don't need shoes and will resist capitalism, be the barefoot King. It's my Coat of One Colour that matters, regal purple, Christ's passion, suffering and sexual pleasure, I need to be *inviolate*—Joseph's brothers persecuted him for the Coat of Many Colours, mark of distinction, chosen one of his father.

Headlights comfort me as I run: a Sunday school fable says patches of light around the world are slowly pooling and soon everyone will glow. I can run on the pavement but the earth is much softer. We could eliminate roads at the same time as shoes. I splash ankle-deep in the puddles.

Entering the grounds of the University, I meet a classmate who says, "How you doin', Jade? You've got your shoes off."

"I know."

"What are you doing?"

"I'm K-ing the campus."

"Cleaning?" he says.

"No, K-ing. I was King, but I reject hierarchy. I'm K-ing until Nott comes. Then he and I will be OK and we'll OK the campus."

"Can I buy you a beer?"

"I only drink water now." You can't buy me. I make for the square pillar, a Native Indian sculpture, that stands outside the library, planning to dance around it until other people join me. Then we can dance around it holding hands. As a shape that naturally arises from the earth, a pillar shouldn't frighten us. Neither should the gates to the exclusive neighbourhood called The Uplands. They're posts with circular lights on top, they're upside down exclamation marks that shout with joy over the space between them—for there is no barrier, anyone can enter and enjoy the green beauty.

I begin to circle the pillar, then realize that it's not my job to create a ring: the University is already shaped by the Ring Road, the city planners have already said it. Around a cauldron, a gallows, a pyre of burning books, a closed circle can terrify. But the Ring Road is not hermetic; it's intersected at many points by other streets. And at the centre, the University. All together.

I no longer walk, I gravitate. The University Centre draws me in.

There's a French psychoanalyst who says that everyone must line up in front of one bathroom door or the other; for Lacan, no human subject exists outside the division into two sexes. But a third door exists between the two in the University Centre: the door to the janitor's supply room. It stands open, light streaming out, while the custodian, arms folded, watches the room from his chair across the hall (Latin: *custos*=guard). Keys dangle from the ring on his belt. I approach him. "This is going to sound crazy, but I've been walking around outside with my shoes off, and there're no paper towels in the women's washroom to dry my feet with." He starts forward and fetches me some without a word. Now the next step becomes clear: having given the password, enter. I open one of the series of heavy wooden doors off the foyer and step into the auditorium.

Tinkling music, all bells and harp, floats across the dark theatre from the small circle of musicians on the stage. Sliding into a seat on the aisle, I notice a lone man with silver glasses hunched in the seat behind me. "Is this a rehearsal?" I whisper. "No, it's my piece," he says. "But they all wrote a piece of it, right?" He looks puzzled and says, "No, it's *my* piece." "Then what's the difference?" I ask. "What do you mean?" "Between playing and writing?" He raises an eyebrow, puts his finger to his lips and says, "Shh." Ah! He's just posing as devil's advocate. The conductor starts forward with a jerk. At this signal, I rise, speed through the theatre and mount the stage. I pick up a cellist's music and she says, "Hey, that's *my* music!" "But you can play without it—play! Look at that, it says 'Fandance.' That's only one arbitrary signifier away from Candance—we can all dance, and anyone who says can't is full of cant. We can't keep this in, the bird has flown." Magic wand in hand, the conductor approaches and touches my shoulder. "I think it has too, but we're not ready for you yet. Would you please go with this man." I am being taken into the bosom of the community, I am the one in the Purple Coat, the one they've been waiting for. A stalwart trumpeter (giver of the Judgement Day clarion call, *dies irae*) ushers me off to the wings. We step backstage into the twisting, well-ordered corridors of the University's heart. Warm-Up Room. "This is where we should go because I'm cold. But wait: if you go alone into a room with a man he can rape you—can we leave the door open? I'm scared of the closed door." My escort props open the door. Outside the window, cars circle the Ring, their lights irradiating the mist: all the spies have joined my side. I slip off my coat and lay it across the piano bench. A gentle glow suffuses the room—I recline on the floor and let it envelop me. My escort sits on the window sill. Slowly, I yield to the pulsions traversing me. My legs slightly spread, my arms above my head, my hips thrusting as I talk, I am being cleansed of my shame, purified from the inside. The Light rolls over me, ripples through me. "I'm afraid of the gun." The bullet will come after they've coaxed my jouissance out of me: this is the female power they can't afford to have publicized.

"What gun?"

"The gun in your pocket."

"What, this?" he says in surprise, and pulls out his sheet music to show me the dancing black notes.

"I see, that's a fluid river to delight me, not a bullet to kill me." My spirit has expanded to fill my skin; I inhabit my body thoroughly, comfortably. I stand up and do a walkover to show how flexible my identity is. My shirt slips down to half-expose my breasts. Arched in a bridge I say, "See, I can come up either way." I right myself. "I can come up like this." I bend backwards again, this time kicking my legs over my head in a back-walkover, "Or like this." I lie back down and raise my legs perpendicularly, ankles together. "My next-door neighbour used to have feet like moccasins during the summer. She could stand on a big rock and jump down onto the little ones and it wouldn't hurt her." Then I see it: "That's the point, isn't it, just to be one of the little rocks." My escort approaches and kneads my bare feet. "My feet aren't very hard yet," I apologize. His touch lingers, then withdraws.

It's time to go to the bathroom again. He takes me to another set of three doors. "I know I could go in the middle, but I'm not ready to pee on the floor yet." To my relief, he agrees, "No, that would be bad."

By the time we return to the concert hall, the conductor and musicians have disappeared and my escort sets about clearing the stage. I crouch on the stairs. "Are you Gabriel?" I ask.

"My name is Terry," he says, stacking chairs.

"Are you sure you're not Gabriel? You know, the guardian angel from the Bible? Are you married to Gabri-elle?"

"Is she in the Bible too?"

"Do you know her?"

"No."

"Why not?"

"I haven't met her yet."

Will I have to sleep with Terry, then? He squats on a step below me and I study his potato-like face. I crumple inside, I'm too little, I don't want to. The trunk of my body hollows out. My tear ducts squirt.

A jury of angels hovers in the seats of the auditorium. They send a golden cloud pressing into me—it swallows me, smothers me. I grip my head and choke. "No!" The pulsing yellow pressure on my temples lets up. Relief pours over me like clear water: no one is going to force me.

Terry has finished tidying the stage and says he has to teach a trumpet lesson. He holds his instrument at his side, in a black case. I am reluctant to let him go, but he insists. The angels disperse as he extinguishes the lights, and we leave the dark theatre. Outside, the night is thick, but lampposts people the campus, whispering rumours into the dark. We walk together until we reach another building. I say, "I guess I'll go in here." "Are you sure you'll be all right?" he asks, and, gathering my strength, I say, "Yes." The door yields with a friendly click when I tug.

I lie down on a bench in the hallway, shut my eyes, and talk to the immortals telepathically. "You mean you have a partner, but you only get together with that partner sometimes? And when you do, you don't have to have sex, but only sometimes? Just spending time with your partner is a refreshing rest?" Several small, floating faces nod enthusiastically. I'm giggling to myself when an immortal approaches down the hallway. Her bobbed hair bounces around her shoulders and she hugs an armload of books to her chest. "Excuse me, but are you all right?" she says in a voice full of mock concern.

"If someone's laughing by themselves, there's supposed to be something wrong with them!"

Her face blurs with nodding. "Everyone knows it's more fun to share the joke."

Share the joke. My summons has come.

MENTAL HEALTH ACT

PART 3

ADMISSION AND DETENTION OF PATIENTS

Emergency Procedures

24. (1) Where a police officer or constable is satisfied from his own observations or from information received by him that a person

(a) is acting in a manner likely to endanger his own safety or that of others; and

(b) is apparently suffering from mental disorder, he may take the person into custody and take him immediately to a physician; and if the physician is satisfied that that person is a mentally disordered person and in need of care, supervision or control for his own protection or welfare or for the protection of others, he may be taken, on the certificate of the physician, to a Provincial mental health facility, a psychiatric unit or an observation unit; otherwise he shall be released.

JADE

Consummation: I burst from the building and part the low fog that veils the campus as I charge Clearihue. I climb the corner staircase with its glass-panelled landings, to the third floor, and turn the corner. A woman professor steps from her office, blue eyes glowing and a soft, knowing smile on her lips. I march to Duncan's open door and leap into his lap. We beam at each other. His freckles stand out, marks of Pan, animal skin-spots, natural and good, like bare feet.

"Do you want to go for a walk?" he says.

"We could stay here."

"Not with my colleague down the hall."

I slump with fatigue. I thought it was my turn for the refreshing partner-rest the immortals spoke of, but if he still thinks we've got something to hide, then he needs to achieve further revelations. "OK," I sigh, "we'll go for a walk."

In the hallway, he notices my feet padding along the linoleum. "Where are your shoes?"

"I know where they are."

As we proceed into the Centre, he eyes me suspiciously. "You're looking very—" but he can't find the word. "Let's find your shoes, Jade." I approach the empty newspaper box and look in: "Are they in the *Martlet* box? Nope! They're not in there!" *Why do you want to clip my wings?*

We climb the steps to the mezzanine floor of the Centre. "Do you want to consummate our love or just drink consommé? And how do you spell it?" *The "u" can be stabbed or raped; the "o" is protected.*

"What are you on, anyways?" He sinks into a wall-side cushion and I straddle his lap again.

"I'm on you."

"Of course, and I'm on a cube cushion. No, really."

"I'm on water. Do you want to see where I got it? Are you thirsty?"

"Not for water," he says glibly, sliding his hands up my thighs.

I back away in terror. "You want to drink my water?" To consume me? *Consummate me* comes the voice. *Consume ate me.* "I thought my work was done." But I take a breath, struggling to master my fear. "Let me show you where I get my water."

"I've already seen it," he says, but he follows me down to the foyer. A private eye in a trenchcoat and bowler hat holds a briefcase and looks out the window, trying to appear inconspicuous. I know everything I say is being taped and understood. *"Déjà? Ou deva? Et pourquoi? ¿Por qué?"* I try my best to speak a mumbo-jumbo of languages, to recreate Babel. The spy stifles a smile. Meanwhile Duncan says, "One hundred and forty-seven. That's an existentialist principle. Any question can be answered with a number."

I drink from the fountain. He's beginning to catch on. "You don't know the answer to every question."

"I know you'll be going to the bathroom in an hour," he replies. "Well, I'm going back to *Clearihue*." I grin with relief, reading this as, "Clear: I/you." He has recognized his place at my side in the revolution unfolding tonight. He escapes just in time.

In come the Boys in Blue, first security guards, then police officers. The interrogation begins. I freely dispense name, student number, and address, adding, "Yeah, you should check out my house." My head half-cocked, I nod slowly and let a sly smile spread across my face, picturing the collage of relics I have left strewn on the kitchen counter: *Contemporary American Poetry* open to Ginsberg's "Howl"; my opal ring; a sheet of paper listing the etymologies of my family's names . . . . "Would you like me to dance?" I ask, drag-stepping, arms in a broad 'V.' "I can do jazz, ballet, or tap." I skip among the coffee tables and ashtrays. "You can learn anything you want," I tell the security guard. "You can become anything you want."

"So life is a dream, is that what you're telling me?"

"Yes!"

"Do you want me to call your parents?" He wishes to include them in the excitement.

"By all means. Unfurl the red carpet and bring in the Kings!" Grey-haired and bespectacled, he scurries off as fast as his short, stout legs will carry him.

"Sit down, Jade," a sprightly, bearded police officer says.

His partner leers with woman-hating eyes. I say, "Would you like me to sit down?" *You can't order me around because I want to oblige you.*

"Yes."

"K." I sink into a cube cushion.

"What's your name again?" He stands before me, pen poised over a pocket-sized notebook. "Jade King?"

"No. My parents are Kings. I am K-ing. Like OK-ing. Only I need nought to be OK." I make a circle with my thumb and forefinger to show that nought is the "O" in OK.

"What's that?"

As I repeat the mantra, it changes meaning. "I need nought to be OK. I need Nott to be okay. I need not to be okay." To convey these messages to the police officer demands concentrated effort. I recite them with varied intonations until at last understanding blooms behind his eyes.

"Jade, your parents are here," the security guard comes puffing to announce.

"It's okay, Jade, go with your parents," the officer says.

"I need not to be okay."

"Go with your parents," he insists.

"But I *need* not-to-be-okay."

Mom's face jars me with its familiarity. Her off-white jacket stands out like a blotch of cream. Dad, a dark pillar in his long raincoat, melts into the walls. I give in, concluding that they must need me, and that now the police force will carry on my work. I crawl into the brown plush of the sedan and shut the door.

At home Mom puts a plate of spaghetti in front of me. I stare at the foreign matter from far away, pick at it, then beat a retreat to my room. Thinking to outfox them, I lock my door (this door which locks from the inside) and fly out my bedroom window (this window without bars). They're on to me.

"I don't want to chase you, Jade."

"I don't want you to chase me, Dad." It's out of hand, out of their hands.

Since I have already K'ed the campus, I wander for awhile with less urgency, wondering what to tackle next. The Student Union Building houses a pub that trades in beer and sex: the patrons need educating, but they're liable to misunderstand and harm me. I flex my spirit and accost the SUB. At once the cops surround me again. I can't trust all of them, not all pigs can be changed, not all by me—the leering misogynist is here—but his sprightly partner is gone—oh no! I drink some more water. "Can I talk to you in private?" the cop says to me.

The closed door terrifies me. I will be raped and shot. My instinct says to keep people around me. I enter a room where some students have gathered around a table, the SUB Upper Lounge. "Is it anything you can't say in front of my friends?" He's speechless. Back out in the foyer I shout, "You want to FUCK me don't you?" He smirks—how could any woman touch that bastard?

Bravely, I descend the stairs into the bar—Felicita's, place of happiness and good fortune according to the Latinate root—but I am on trial for my sexuality. I am fighting through the dance in a sexual battle. They send the pig down. He takes a ringside seat, leaning on the bar, speaking into his walkie-talkie.

Marilyn Monroe's essence seeps into me and I live her torturous experience—the sex idol that all the men wanted, forced to flaunt her body in front of them—for I jazz dance by myself. Convention forbids women to dance for their own pleasure, they might be practising pagan rites. The cop continues to smirk, waiting for me to strip, like the dancers he watches in other bars. He doesn't understand the joy of movement, can't separate physicality from his pornographic notion of sex—he probably even thinks I want him.

I summon courage and approach the cop. "I'd like to buy this man a glass of water," I tell the bartender. He pours one out. "How much?" I ask. "Aren't you going to let me pay for it?" CAN'T YOU SEE? I think, YOU CAN'T BUY WATER, I AM (composed of at least 90%) WATER ERGO YOU CAN'T CONSUME ME. The cop doesn't get it. He's beginning to understand, however, that I don't want him, with his damned extraneous phallus hanging from his belt. "I don't want to close any doors with you, sir." His sneer promises retribution. Beer bottles and cigarette butts overflow the tables; the laughter of the crowd swells to a derisive roar. I race back upstairs.

More cops. My parents returned. "Jade, your parents want you to go home with them."

"Again? I've already gone home!" It's my passing presence that matters, I think. The K-ing Midas touch. But no. They want to take me into a room. "No! You'll close the door!" And I know what will happen. I'll be raped and shot, out of disappointment, because to sleep with a goddess always disappoints—that's why they killed Marilyn: deceptive vessel; promised, perfect piece of cunt.

A new cop wants to take me into a room this time. I remember the taboo that will save me: the incest taboo, displaced a little, but surely no one would have sex with me in front of my parents. I enter the room with the familiar security guard, my parents, and the new cop—a thirtyish man with sandy-brown hair and the obligatory handlebar moustache. A blonde girl wearing scholar's glasses and carrying books against her chest bursts in: "Yes? What's going on? This is my office." She doesn't even look at me, the cause of all the commotion. "There are too many people in here," says the cop. My dad picks up his cue. "I'm the father here," he says, putting his hand on the girl's shoulder—as if he were *her* father! I protest his leaving, fearing I will be shut up with the Boys in Blue after all. "Your mom is here, is that all right?" the cop says, and I turn around—there she is in her cream-coloured coat, with that echoing face. "Okay," I say. He instructs me to sit down while he stands in front of me with crossed arms.

"What's on your hip?" I ask in terror.

"Pants," he says.

"What else?"
"A belt."
"What else?"
"A holster."
"But what's inside the holster? A gun!"
"I don't have the authority to use it."
"You have a gun for shooting people. Who's in charge here?"
"I am."
"Didn't you just say you didn't have the authority?"
His face softens, he almost smiles.
"Phone Dr. Nott," I say to the security guard behind the desk. "He understands me."
"Is he a professor at the university?"
"Yes, yes, he has his Ph.D."
The guard flips pages in the phone book, then dials. I stand up and yell, "Duncan Nott I need you now, I'm dead serious! You need me too! Dun Cannot! We need each other to be OK!" If I show that I have a partner, then maybe I won't be raped and shot. It is time for Duncan and me to come together: our bodies' meeting will ignite the new sexual revolution—but without his help, I will be killed. "I'm dead serious, Duncan!"

I take my chair. "What is this place called?" I ask the cop.
"The SUB," he says.
"How do you spell that?"
"S-U-B."
"What do you get if you invert those letters?"
"B-U-S. Bus."

"Is there a bus stop around here?" I ask.

"Yes, there's one just over there," he says.

"But where is it? It's right on top of the SUB, isn't it? Invert SUB and you get bus. Now, do you know what 'bus' is short for?"

"No, I'm just a dumb cop," he says, shifty-eyed.

"I'll tell you. It's short for *omnibus*. Do you know what omnibus means in Latin?"

"No."

"It's the dative plural meaning 'for all.' The bus is for all, the SUB is for all."

His eyes veritably twinkle. "You'd make a great defence lawyer."

I sigh. "Now can I rest?"

"No, Jade," he says, assuming his business face again, "you're a danger to yourself. You were crossing the street in front of cars—"

"But what happened before I crossed?" He shakes his head as if to say, No more fun and games. "The cars stopped! I waited for them to stop!"

He turns to my mother. "I'm sorry, ma'am, but we can't apprehend her unless she's being a danger to herself or others."

I have won. We have won. Duncan and I. He is to meet me in front of the SUB. Set free, I stroll outside to wait, longing to be alone with Duncan, but my guardians follow me. I say, "Come on, I'll introduce you to Duncan Nott." As I cross the Ring Road tailed by my parents, I see Duncan walking hand in hand with a woman, then the couple disintegrates before my eyes.

We follow the cement path beside Clearihue. Light burns in a third floor office—Duncan's light. We climb the stairs and I prance to his door. I knock but receive no answer. As I press myself into the door, kissing it, the heavy cold surface begins to yield. Duncan's lips respond to mine and his erection bumps my pelvis. I rock my hips playfully. His flesh becomes warmer and warmer, the door between us, thinner and thinner. "Don't you see, we can cleanse the doors of perception like Blake said, it's our duty." I jiggle the clitoral door knob. "It's okay, we can do it in front of my parents." *There's nothing more natural, we can defeat the Oedipal obsession.* He presses harder in response but still says nothing—they've got him gagged and bound, they're in there saying, *Show us. Prove it.* The Devil asks Christ why he doesn't jump off a cliff if he truly has faith in God. I falter. I have known the faith-driven strain of Duncan's passion against the door, and have given myself in return. Now what? I turn my head—my parents have their backs to me and are retreating down the hall. Hallelujah!

"That's it! There's no need for incest because Harold and Harriet are one! Harold and Harriet are one!" I yell, stepping back from the door, flinging my arms ceiling-ward. "I can give you a blow-job, Dad! I can suck you off—but I don't want to! I don't want to!" Free of Freud, I run to my father and fall to my knees before him. I bob my head and a phallus made of compressed, golden air like a halo penetrates me. I am ministering to my Father. The human one starts to hit me hard on the head, *wap*, *wap*, *wap*, from side to side.

"Yes, you can hit me Dad, I don't care!" because my synapses won't register pain—pain becomes ecstatic abasement in the service of the Lord.

Blankness.

When awareness returns, I am shooting the breezeway of the Centre, vaulting the stairs and scaling an upside-down exclamation mark, squealing with joy: "We don't have to be afraid of the phallic signifiers!" My Beloved and I work our magic. His lips press mine. I close my eyes, hugging him, legs wrapped around him, waiting for our force to conjure him, for him to emerge from inside the pillar. Fevered, naked, I pant and groan and writhe and strain towards my incorporeal lover and "Jade," I hear. With reluctance, I open my eyes. Clothes materialize around my limbs. I am prostrate on the sidewalk beside a lamppost. My Beloved has slipped away again. His spirit gleams whitely in the dot of the exclamation mark.

"Can you hear me, Jade? You have to come with me. Do you understand what I'm saying to you?" This is the friendly cop in whom I have awakened the divine, and beyond him, a woman waits—his partner. But behind their vehicle idles another police car. What he is saying, as he speaks slowly, weighting his words with emphasis, is, there's no way out, come with me because I am here to help you fulfill your mission in bridging the gap. Come with me because the next car holds ordinary cops—we are decoys, and immortals take care of their own.

I rise and get into the back of the car with the lady

cop. "I feel like I'm in God's arms," I say, relaxing into the seat, finally allowed to rest for awhile.

We arrive at the Emergency Ward of the hospital. I don't get dragged in kicking and screaming; I walk in between the policepeople. "I think I have to go to the bathroom." They lead me to a small, tiled room and start to close the door. "No! Don't close the door!" I cry. "Come in here with me." The woman decoy in her steel-toed boots giggles and says, "I don't want to watch you go to the bathroom." I am not afraid of her because I believe she won't rape me. "I *need* you to keep an eye on me," I plead. "I need you to hold the door." Her brown eyes soften when she smiles.

I kneel in front of the toilet. Now I think I need to throw up. "I need you to hold my hair back like my mom does." I vomit into the bowl and a nurse appears at my side. "What did you eat tonight, Jade?" "Spaghetti—with a little bit of hot sauce," I say, and somebody giggles, the elfish voices giggle. My face is roughly licked by a warm face cloth. I am led out again, this has only been a warm-up, a not-so-dry run. "I don't want to go back in the car." The male cop says, "Is it all right if you go with her?" I recognize my female friend and say, "Can we leave the door open?" He says yes, and as I get into the car on one side, the door on the other side is open, all four doors stand open at once, like wings. Then they are closed: I've been tricked, where are they taking me? I don't want to go home, the drama/trauma isn't over yet. "I think I've cottoned on to something, and I don't want to keep it all to myself!"

I cry, tossing my head from side to side against the seat. "I think I've caught-onned on to something." It's vital that they hear the difference in the sameness. Salvation depends on my inflection.

— im stretched out on my back again   eyes closed i thinknow my arms are being held out (like in those cults where they make people perform sex) but this is on American/national tv (it had to end up there) there are a circle of people around me with cameras and flashcubes and movie lights (i do not fear the Light) i can hear them marvelling at this event   i know Mick Jagger and David Bowie and the Clintons are watching i am ripe for my lover and he is kneeling naked and hard on the floor right in front of me   and we are straining towards each other with a pure gold longing but we dont do it   we wont do it   even though its obvious how much we want it my breath storms   my pelvis thrusts   my back arches   im tantalized by ethereal foreplay brought within seconds of orgasm my lover poised inches away   but we wont do it for fame or profit every time im about to come the messages change   i say "i think i have to throw up" or "i think i have to pee" and everybody laughs they must be hearing "i think i have to come" because that would be funny to American national tv this is when Marilyn really pervades me   i know i appear as the naked Marilyn   trying to show there are some things that cant be bought   i keep being swept to the verge of orgasm but my body declines it   until finally they pack up their cameras and

| 71

leave i can hear their shoes clicking down the hall as their voices die away done with the public sphere the joke becomes serious and the drama personal and holy im in the bathroom on the floor "Now you kneel in front of her" they say to a man in black pants and im lying in the same position as before still looking like marilyn (goddess incarnate) my platinum blonde hair gleaming waves pound me with the force of the surf Diana chaste goddess of the moon and my water-filled body using me to breach the gap between Venus and herself the virgin/whore opposition is being dismantled in MY body i am being cleansed from the inside with holy waves "O O O" my voice keens my hips are pumping the golden phallus plunges through vagina rectum bladder stomach scouring me inside out showing me i have nothing to fear from this temple i inhabit familiar muscle contractions are triggered my guts heave i spew and retch leaking warm fluid as i vomit and urinate at once exquisite post-orgasmic relief for a few seconds then the pulsating strokes start again orgasm really does become vomiting pleasure becomes pain theres a crucial distinction but its circular and the shortest verse in the Bible is "Jesus wept" time is relative pain shrinks but oh multiple orgasm is SO tiring the waves start crashing on me again i can hear the immortals giggling when my eyes are closed but they are still cradling me they revere the goddess in me when i open my eyes i see heads "It's OK, Jade" they say "can i stop now?" i beg "Just one more, Jade," a voice says sweetly its up to me to survive this crucifixion theyre nailing my flesh to the wall my powder blue eyes widen with the anguish of coming/dying and meanwhile Duncan still hovers above me afraid to thrust inside me waiting to be convinced that its all right for them to say "It's OK, Duncan" i see his flattered bafflement "She can't want me" hes thinking "I'm not worthy, I don't want to contaminate a goddess" he cant believe hes allowed to fuck Marilyn she's a poster on a wall but the hospital staff/votaries are now urging him to do it and im pleading with my body this isnt just lust boy its the redemption of humankind to fuck only for the perfect unity of reasons physical intellectual emotional but above all social and spiritual satisfaction and good "Do this for the good of society, you two, here in the privacy of your own room—we know you can't be bought, what the two of you are bringing to the world between you can't be bought"

    ive already slept with Jesus when i was 14 in my dream i was a whore in a special brothel set up for Jesus and his disciples for their sexual satisfaction on the road and Jesus picked me and we went into a closet much like this tiny bathroom and he knelt before me in his robe i dont remember penetration but he definitely deflowered me still the spiritual phallus is not enough because Duncan remains behind the screen of his own unknowing until finally we do cleanse the doors of perception/ break on through to the other side Duncan bursts into corpo-reality and Jesus is embodied in him because hes always already inside of all of us this time the union is real love can be startling breath-stealing

*almost brutally passionate slam-bam but true
unbounded free revel of flesh   juicy squelch   scratch of
pubic hair but sacred   holy and whole   i jerk forward
eyes and mouth pop open and i gasp with the pleasure
of shock   a new sensation like a jump into icy emerald-
green river-water   you are where your dreams take you
ive been to heaven and back   finally fulfilled the
prophecy   we are* OK *we did it for Jesus/for the good of
society   the Marriage of the Lamb*

« 4 »

—Did you ever do anything wild when you were younger?

—Let's see. Well, there was one time. I sure paid for it the next day. It was my graduation night. Some of the fellows had got hold of some beer and they talked me into drinking with them, I wasn't used to it. I guess I had a reputation for being pretty straight-laced. Anyway, I gave in and drank six bottles. Then they dared me to climb up the water tower and paint GRAD '48. The reservoir was sort of a round hut with a cone-shaped roof—only it was on very tall stilts. Boy it was high! I would never have had the guts to climb it sober, yet here I was carrying a bucket and a brush and swaying up there in the dark, painting letters as big as the sweep of my arm. Looking back, I'm surprised I didn't get myself killed. The trip back down is a blank. All I know is next morning I woke up in a ditch with the worst migraine of my life. It made me swear off drinking forever. That was my one and only binge.

HISTORY

GVHS
ROYAL JUBILEE HOSPITAL

KING, Jade
#00628343
DR. R. YOUNGER

cc: Dr. P. Montgomery

ADMISSION DIAGNOSIS: Acute manic state.

HISTORY OF PRESENT ILLNESS: This 21-year-old patient of Dr. Montgomery's present in the Emergency Department at 2345 hours with the Saanich Police. The police gave a story that they brought her here from the University where she was behaving bizarrely. They had initially apprehended her at the request of her parents in the University dorm where she was engaged in a group sexual situation. She was taken home but subsequently locked her bedroom door and climbed out the window. She was again found on the University campus and on the second occasion was sexually stimulating herself against a telephone pole. When the police arrived she lay on the grass and was masturbating herself. She subsequently removed her clothing and continued the masturbation activity. The police apprehended her and brought her to the Emergency Department. The parents state that the patient has deteriorated over the past three days only and has been a good student and had no previous history of problems prior to this. In the past three days, however, she has not been sleeping and has had increasingly bizarre behaviour with increased talking and a general uncooperative state. Her speech has become somewhat bizarre with unconnected ideas and general irritability.

The patient states that there is no family history of any depressive illness or unipolar depressive illness. The patient's mother has one uncle who died under mysterious circumstances but she is not aware that there was suicide.

PAST MEDICAL HISTORY: Good.
MEDICATIONS: None.
ALLERGIES: None known.

PSYCHIATRIC ASSESSMENT: The patient is in the psychiatric examination room and has vomited two or three times. I did not observe this vomiting behaviour but the police felt that it was self-induced. She has vomitus on her face and in her hair and is making no effort to clean herself up. She is lying on the floor and partly blocking the door. She does not remove herself from the door when requested. She looks quite fatigued and has limited speech. Her responses to questions are inappropriate and she has some bursts of speech with some pressure and some loose connection of words and thoughts.

I am unable to assess her detailed thought content, insight, and or judgement.

IMPRESSION: Acute psychosis, probable manic state. This patient clearly is in need of a protective environment. She is admitted to the psychiatric intensive care unit of the Eric Martin Pavilion on a committal basis. Dr. Lamm was notified of the admission for Dr. Montgomery. The psychiatry rotation is not available in the Emergency Department or in the Eric Martin Pavilion. We called the psychiatrist on call from the previous evening, Dr. Ritchie, and he does not know who the psychiatrist on call after midnight is, nor does he have a rotation, nor does he wish to continue to be on call. We attempted to call Dr. Johnson, the chief of psychiatry, and there was no answer at his home number. The Eric Martin Pavilion is continuing to attempt to find out who the psychiatrist on call is. In the meantime, Dr. Lamm has been given overview of the patient and will assume the care.

DR. R. YOUNGER

MENTAL HEALTH ACT

Involuntary admissions

20. (1) On receipt of 2 medical certificates completed by 2 physicians in accordance with subsection (3), the director of a Provincial mental health facility may admit a person to the facility and detain him in it.

CERTIFICATION IMPLEMENTED

DATE: FEB 29
TIME: 23:45 HR

Province of British Columbia
Ministry of Health

MENTAL HEALTH ACT
(Sections 20(3), 23, 24, and 25, R.S.B.C. 1979, c.256)

PATIENT INFORMED: YES ☑

MEDICAL CERTIFICATE

I, the undersigned __ROBERT ANDREW YOUNGER__
(physician's name in full)

hereby certify that I am a duly qualified medical practitioner of the Province of British Columbia and in the actual practice of the medical profession and that I am not disqualified from giving a valid medical certificate for this person for the reasons set forth in Section 20(4) of the Act.

I examined __JADE LOUISE KING__ on the __29__ of __FEBRUARY__
(person's name in full) (day) (month) (year)

and in my opinion he is mentally disordered. It is also my opinion that __JADE LOUISE KING__
(person's name in full)

requires medical treatment in a facility and care, supervision and control in a facility for his own protection or welfare or for the protection of others.

The reasons, in summary form, upon which my opinion that this person is mentally disordered is founded, are as follows:

__Bizarre behaviour. Total change in character. Hyper-sexual. Pressure of speech. Not sleeping.__

This person was ☑ / was not ☐ brought to me by a police officer or constable under the provisions of section 24(1) of the Act.

Physician's signature: __A. Younger__   Date: __Feb. 29__
P.O. Address: __401-3966 Ashgrove Cres.__   Telephone: __658-1442__

EMERGENCY ADMISSION
(Mental Health Act, section 23)

I certify that, in accordance with section 23 of the Act, there is no other physician who is qualified to give a second medical certificate, by whom this person can be examined, who practices in this vicinity or within a reasonable distance of where this person resides.

Signature of physician _____

NOTE: This medical certificate becomes invalid on the 15th clear day after the date upon which the physician examined the person who is the subject of this certificate.

Improper completion of this form may invalidate the admission procedure.
Please take care in completing the certificate.

Involuntary admission should be used only if the patient cannot be appropriately admitted as an informal patient.

HLTH 3502 (MHS 502) REV. 84/02

CERTIFICATION IMPLEMENTED

DATE MAR 1
TIME 1930

PATIENT INFORMED: YES (Sections 20(1), 23, 24, and 25, R.S.B.C. 1979, c.256)

Province of British Columbia
Ministry of Health

MENTAL HEALTH ACT

MEDICAL CERTIFICATE

I, the undersigned **CHARLES JUSTIN BURNS**
(physician's name in full)

hereby certify that I am a duly qualified medical practitioner of the Province of British Columbia and in the actual practice of the medical profession and that I am not disqualified from giving a valid medical certificate for this person for the reasons set forth in Section 20(4) of the Act.

I examined **JADE LOUISE KING** on the **1st** of **MARCH**
(person's name in full) (day) (month) (year)

and in my opinion he is mentally disordered. It is also my opinion that **JADE LOUISE KING**
(person's name in full)

requires medical treatment in a facility and care, supervision and control in a facility for his own protection or welfare or for the protection of others.

The reasons, in summary form, upon which my opinion that this person is mentally disordered is founded, are as follows:

In manic psychotic state without insight. Represents a danger to herself and others.

This person was ☒ was not ☐ brought to me by a police officer or constable under the provisions of section 24(1) of the Act.

Physician's signature: _____
P.O. Address: 202-1400 Fort St, Victoria, B.C.
Date: 1 MARCH
Telephone: 592-1818

EMERGENCY ADMISSION
(Mental Health Act, section 23)

I certify that, in accordance with section 23 of the Act, there is no other physician who is qualified to give a second medical certificate, by whom this person can be examined, who practices in this vicinity or within a reasonable distance of where this person resides.

Signature of physician _____

NOTE: This medical certificate becomes invalid on the 15th clear day after the date upon which the physician examined the person who is the subject of this certificate.

Improper completion of this form may invalidate the admission procedure.
Please take care in completing the certificate.

Involuntary admission should be used only if the patient cannot be appropriately admitted as an informal patient.

HLTH 3502 (MHS 502) REV. 84/02

MENTAL HEALTH ACT

Deemed consent

25.2 Where a person is detained in a Provincial mental health facility under section 20, 23, 24, 25, 25.1 or 36 . . . treatment authorized by the director shall be deemed to be given with the consent of the person.

Province of British Columbia
Ministry of Health

MENTAL HEALTH ACT

(Sections 20, 23, 24 or 25)

CONSENT FOR TREATMENT, INVOLUNTARY PATIENT

I, _____TERESA BLACK_____
(name of patient, director or officer in charge)

authorize the following treatment(s) with respect to __Jade King__
(name of patient)

at __R.J.H. - Eric Martin Pavilion__
(name of facility)

__TALKING THERAPIES AND MEDICATIONS.__

The nature of the condition, the reasons for and the likely consequence(s) of the treatment(s) have been explained to me by

_____
(name)

Complete either 'A' or 'B'

A. If signed by patient:

Signature of patient:

_____

Date _____ Time _____

Witness _____

To the best of my judgment, the above named patient was capable of understanding the nature of the above authorization at the time it was signed.

_____ M.D.

B. If not signed by patient:

Signature:
J. Black R.N.
(director or officer in charge of facility, or designate)

Position: __B.C.N.__

Date: __01 March__

Witness: _____

The above named patient is an involuntary patient (sections 20, 23, 24 or 25 *Mental Health Act*) and to the best of my judgment is incapable of appreciating the nature of the treatment and/or his need for it and is therefore incapable of giving consent.

_____ M.D.

HLTH 3510 (MHS 510) REV. 84/02

MENTAL HEALTH ACT

Direction and discipline of patient

26. Every patient detained in the Provincial mental health facility is, during detention, subject to the direction and discipline of the director and the members of the staff of the Provincial mental health facility authorized in that behalf by the director.

PIC (Psychiatric Intensive Care): I

A votary leads me to the bathing chamber and divests me of my garments. At her touch, steaming fluid gushes from a silver faucet into an ivory tub. She offers me decanters of frankincense and myrrh, but I need only water to purify myself. As the level rises, vapour clouds the room. I enter my private pool.

Alone, I perform my ablutions. With a cloth, I stroke my arms. When I lie back to immerse my head, water buoys my hair into a corona. I feel sleek and beautiful inside my skin, my round breasts high on my chest, my nipples rosy pink. "She's in there having a bath, you can go look at her," I hear through the open door.

"No, I don't want to look at her," Duncan replies.

From the mist, I emerge reborn. My handmaiden helps me dress. As I leave the vestry, a waiting woman opens crimson lips and sings as if underwater, "She's preparing for her Bridegroom." A large group rejoices in slow motion as I pass into the bridal suite. I disrobe and slip under the bedcovers. When I close my eyes,

Duncan's steady breathing rises from the pillow beside me. I inhale more deeply to keep time with the rhythm of his larger lungs, and drift to sleep.

When I awake I have to urinate. I try the door but it's locked. I knock. "Excuse me sir, or ma'am? Excuse me please. I have to go to the bathroom." Knock knock knock. "Please let me out. I have to go to the bathroom and if you don't let me out, I'll have to go in here." A jangling of keys affirms this proposal. "But I can't go in here, there's no toilet!" I scan the room in vain for bucket, bowl, or cup. "I see. You need me to pee on the floor." They need to be liberated from the oppression of social conventions, which start with toilet training. I pull my right leg out of my pajama bottoms and they sink to a pool around my left ankle. Planting my feet wide, I clench my fists, close my eyes, and let the torrent of urine gush out of me.

Sunlight wakes me. The stamp on the bedsheet reads "Royal Jubilee Hospital, Eric Martin Pavilion." World liberation is indeed a jubilant occasion.

Keys rattle at the door and a man enters. I cover myself with a blanket, having left my soiled pajamas in a heap. "The floor's rather wet, isn't it?" He returns with a mop and tidies my cell. After he leaves, a woman brings a pair of clean pajamas and stays until I have dressed.

A tall man in a white coat lurches into my room. "I'm Dr. Burns," he announces.

Fire burns providing life-giving warmth—that's a good name. "Can you explain the mess?" The doctor frowns as he gestures to the floor, to my mattress, which has been stripped. I take a breath to explain my symbolic defiance of social norms, but as I examine the hard lines of his face, I check myself.

"I had to go to the bathroom and they wouldn't let me out. I tried to wipe it up."

"Do you know where you are?"

"At the Royal Jubilee Hospital."

"Do you know what area specifically?"

"Yes, I'm in the Eric Martin Pavilion." The same 'Eric Martin' flung about the schoolyard as a taunt all through my childhood.

"Do you remember what happened last night?"

Ah, yes. The consummation, the circle of people with cameras. He's on my side after all. I giggle with relief.

"It's all on film, isn't it?" If it has been filmed, word will spread; I don't have to keep fighting to express it.

"No, it's not on film. Did you use drugs last night or in the past few days?"

"No. I used my own strength."

"To do what?"

"I thought you knew."

"No, I don't know."

"They must have hushed it up."

"Who are 'they'?"

"The authorities."

Dr. Burns leans over his clipboard, his white jacket a

flag of authority. "What is it 'they' might have hushed up? Is there something special about you?" Eyes bugged, pencil poised, he waits to devour my reply.

CONSULTATION KING: Jade
GVHS 628343 PIC EMP
ROYAL JUBILEE HOSPITAL Dr. C.J. Burns
cc: Dr. P. Montgomery

Date of admission: 29 February

The patient was assessed in PIC. She was unable to provide any reliable history. She smiled at the interviewer throughout the interview. She exhibited hyperactivity in getting up and down from her chair repeatedly. Her speech was somewhat pressured. She alluded to various powers but would not discuss these with me. She was suspicious and refused to answer many of the interviewer's questions. Her sensorium appeared clear, although it could not be formally tested. Judgement and insight were grossly impaired.

OPINION:

There is no question whatsoever that this girl deserves a diagnosis of major affective disorder, bipolar, manic, psychotic.

RECOMMENDATIONS:

1. To be treated as an inpatient on an involuntary basis.

2. Lithium carbonate 600 mg t.i.d. initially and this will be prescribed according to clinical response and serum Lithium levels.

3. Haldol 5 mg q.i.d. and p.r.n. and Cogentin 2 mg p.r.n.

4. She will likely require an admission in the order of 2-3 weeks.

The prognosis for her rapid recovery is excellent.

Dr. C.J. Burns

Compendium of Pharmaceuticals and Specialties

HALDOL
Haloperidol
Antipsychotic
…

Indications:
Management of manifestations of acute and chronic psychosis, including schizophrenia and manic states.

Warnings:
… In rare cases, the following symptoms were reported during the concomitant use of lithium and haloperidol: encephalopathy, extrapyramidal symptoms, tardive dyskinesia, neuroleptic malignant syndrome, brain stem disorder, acute brain syndrome and coma. …

Precautions:
… It has been reported that seizures can be triggered by haloperidol. …

Adverse Effects:
Neurological effects are the most common. …In common with all neuroleptics, extrapyramidal symptoms may occur, e.g., tremor, rigidity, hypersalivation…. …As with all antipsychotic agents, tardive dyskinesia may appear in some patients. The syndrome is characterized by rhythmical involuntary movements of the tongue, face, mouth or jaw (e.g. protrusion of tongue, puffing of cheeks, puckering of mouth, chewing movements). Sometimes these may be accompanied by involuntary movements of extremities. The manifestations may be permanent in some patients.

...Other CNS effects: Insomnia, depressive reactions, and toxic confusional states are the more common effects encountered. Drowsiness, lethargy, stupor and catalepsy, confusion, restlessness, agitation, anxiety, euphoria, vertigo, grand mal seizures and exacerbation of psychotic symptoms, including hallucinations, have also been reported. ...

Autonomic: Dry mouth, blurred vision, urinary retention, incontinence, priapism, erectile dysfunctions,... excessive perspiration or salivation, heartburn, and body temperature disregulation have been reported.

Miscellaneous: Cases of sudden and unexpected death have been reported in association with the administration of haloperidol. ...

Reprinted with permission from the Compendium of Pharaceuticals and Specialties. *Copyright 1999 Canadian Pharmacists Association.*

I cross the threshold of my cell and enter a noisy crowd. Smoke and body heat thicken the air. Purgatory? The underworld? The afterlife? If so, I will be reunited with my dead relatives. I slide into a booth opposite a woman whose waist-length hair frames her face with streaks of grey. Her blue eyes assess me as she drags on her cigarette. "Who are you? Are you Louise? Are you my grandmother?" I ask.

"Tell me about your grandmother."

"She used to play the piano at the silent movies when she was a teenager but she didn't get home until late and her parents didn't think it was right for a girl to be running around by herself at night, so she had to stop."

"I like to run around at night," the woman answers. Her eyes entrance me.

"She was born on Hallowe'en and she was superstitious. She left her opal ring to me because it's bad luck for people not born in October to wear them."

"I have an opal ring."

"And what happens when you hold it up to the light?" I ask, cupping my hands together and raising them.

"You can see all the colours of the rainbow," we say together.

"Why don't we go get our rings? Where are they?"

My grandmother averts her gaze. After a pause, she resumes. "You know what my doctor told me? I've been in PIC eighteen times." She emphasizes each syllable by gesturing to the table with her cigarette: *"Eighteen times."*

"Where is the rest of our family? Where's Edgar?"

Again she looks away. Her silence implies that she cannot impart this knowledge to me. But why? It must not be time for me to join my ancestors: my own generation still needs me. I start questing, not for my granddad, but for Duncan.

The hallway extends like the top of a "T" on either side of the lounge. Each wing contains four rooms on a common side of the hall. Most are empty, their doors ajar. I slide open the window-covers of the closed doors, stand on tiptoe and peer in. None of the forms within looks familiar.

At last I arrive at a room with no peep-window. A red button cheekily asserts itself at eye-level beside this door. Below the button, a piece of red tape punched with white block letters admonishes: DO NOT TOUCH. The Button! I knock on the door. "Duncan? Duncan, there's a button out here and it says 'DO NOT TOUCH.' Do you want me to touch it?"

Duncan's voice sings out in reply, "No."

He has just refused to have his clitoris touched but he believes he's saving the world. I can free Duncan from his enslavement. I rip off the "DO NOT TOUCH" decal and press the red disc several times. Ha! I run to the other end of the hall and do the same thing with the Button there. Duncan is free. Then I'm having another internal dialogue with the immortals, saying, "We can do it right out here in front of everyone," and I'm slipping out of my pajama top while they say, "No, it's better to do it in the privacy of your own room, it's the only time you get to be alone and anyway, we don't need you to prove it or perform. We believe you," and they're forcing me into my room.

A young woman in a blue robe beckons to me from the hall, but the nurse says, "No, Jade has to stay in her room until she can learn to behave—"

"—in a more appropriate fashion," I finish for her. "Appropriate fashion," the young woman echoes. "Shock treatment didn't do anything for me either."

"Are you sure you don't want anything to drink, Jade?"

As a joke, I shout, "Semen!" The blue-robed woman giggles and the nurse grins but then the key turns in the lock and the portal slides shut. These actions are not jokes. I'm up and wailing. My pajamas, much too large around the waist, fall to the floor and I kick them off. I strip off my top, cross my arms and circle the small room. "I don't want to wait anymore! I'm tired of waiting." Then I hear it. "I don't have to wait! I'm already wading!" Shin-deep water sloshes against my legs as I pace the room. "Don't you see? This is why Jesus was crying. It's no fun to have a joke and to have to keep it all to yourself. It's no fun to be alone. Jesus died before he could make people understand. I'm going to die, too, I can see that. I want to share the joke!" I yell into the window until condensation bubbles up on the plastic. I'm drowning as they fill up the room with water— I'm also shrinking. Though I'm on tiptoe, I can no longer reach the window. They're raising it higher and higher. I'm going to drown. I turn my back to the door and sink to a squat, my body wracked with sobs for the humanity on the other side of the door. The humanity I haven't been able to save.

But where is my partner in all this? I was never meant to do this all alone.

"Daddy!" Duncan's little girl screams. Glass doors slide open as a woman—his wife—strides into the hospital. "Are you guys here, too?" Duncan asks, surprised and a little sheepish. I hug my knees in my corner by the door. "Yes, they're here. You've met my family; now it's time for you to go meet yours." And I let him go, I let him go. I bless him and release him.

Another victory for Duncan and me, for faith, for society. I crawl onto the mattress. Lear jets whine and rumble to a landing on the roof as celebrities from around the world congregate. Grateful daughters and sons crowd the hospital grounds, chanting and beating tambourines. They urge me to come out and join them, to lead an exodus of inmates from this crazy jail. Their singing roars in my ears like the surf. Eventually it diminishes into the blare of the TV and the laughter of people in the next room. I rest under cool green sheets.

ROYAL JUBILEE HOSPITAL
Victoria, B.C.

24 HOUR SUPPLEMENT

TIME: PATIENT PROBLEMS OR TOPIC	ASSESSMENT, ACTION, OUTCOMES (PRN'S WITH TIME IN RED)
	Took tub bath but came to day area w/ only bathrobe on. Did put pj's on w/ direction to do so. Trying all the doors in PIC. Stated was looking for a friend. Sitting in day area socializing. Easily stimulated by tone of unit. Taken to room to settle. Questioned re events leading to hospital. Able to give some info and then states "I forget". Denies using any non prescribed drugs in past few days.
11:20	Haldol 2 mgm liq ☒ to help settle. Very suspicious of the medication and reluctant to take it. Wouldn't drink the juice. "I don't trust you --- it could be poison."
11:50	Out in day area for lunch. Loud boisterous laughing - ☒ Settled in room pc lunch and slept for period — ☒
15:00	Out in day area. Socializing loud boisterous laughing.
15:15	Haldol 5 mgm liq - ☒ Secluded in room to settle and ↓ Stimulation ———— ☒
1700 Disrobed	Pt. is naked in room. - very euphoric, giggly, no insight.
1845	Haldol 5mg liq p.o. given to help control. Wanting a bath & told she could have one if settled in a half hr. BEP Settled & had her tubbath then

DATE: Mar 1

TIME: PATIENT PROBLEMS OR TOPIC	ASSESSMENT, ACTION, OUTCOMES (PRN'S WITH TIME IN RED)
	up in the day area. Behavior more controlled & is able to keep her clothes on now.
	Easily stimulated by tone of unit & is escalating as evening wears on. Interfering c̄ others & conversation inappropriate.
2200	Behavior overactive & pt ran down hall & pushed emergency buzzer. Secluded for same. SC
2200 To ;help settle	Haldol 5 mg. liq. po given BD
2340	Awake & asking to use BR - allowed up to BR. Heard to void - then thump heard & pt found lying on floor by toilet c̄ L.O.C. & body twitching. Then regained consciousness & asked "Where am I" then seemed to become aware. Then slumped over again - eased to floor c̄ body twitching again. Then after about 15-20 sec. became aware again. Stated "I'm having seizures, help me", and then repeated this episode again. When conscious again assisted to bed. BP 60/40 P33.
2345	Dr. Lamm on call for Dr. Montgomery notified & ordered.
2350	Medical Intern called.
	Pt has bruised & swelling area over L. eye & on L. cheek SC Cold pack applied.
2355	Medical Intern on unit. SC

A naked woman is treading the path of exile from Eden, and she turns her head in my direction. Instead of a left eye, she has cross-bones with a hole, a vortex, at the centre. It gapes larger, then a cone of blackness pans forward, blotting my field of vision. Darkness engulfs me, enters my lungs. Frantic for air, for the inverse, I spring to the door, which is locked from the outside, and knock frantically. The peep-hole opens and a man looks in. "You've got to let me out, I have something important to say." He bows his head; I haven't got it quite right. "It's only that I need to go to the bathroom." He turns the key and releases me. I bolt across the hall.

hot white electric currents itch my brain I pulse with shock writhe belly on the floor my bones vibrate my head burns

"Where the hell am I?"

I open my eyes.

"You're in the hospital. You were banging your head on the floor, Jade. Do you know what's happening?"

"Yes, I'm having seizures. I need you to help me stop having seizures."

A woman in white is holding my wrists as though showing me how to surrender. Cowed, I slink back to my cave. It reeks of death.

"Jade, your parents are here to see you."

At the Kings' behest, I drag myself off my pallet and

stagger from the dungeon. I finger the bump on my forehead. My tongue worries a newly sharp surface: I must have broken a tooth.

Around the corner, mustard-yellow armchairs are arrayed before a glassed-in nurses' station. My parents hold court side by side. "We came to see how you were doing," my mother says.

"This is a torture chamber. This is no way to treat a King."

Mom clenches her jaw. "Jade, you're not a king."

"So now you're disowning me?"

Dad chuckles.

"It's not funny, Harold. Jade, you know what I mean."

"Let's sit on the couch." I slump between my parents, barely conscious. Dad's hands are loosely folded in his lap, and his right thumb twitches compulsively. I reach down to stop it.

"What do you want down there?"

"Your hand. Just your hand." I clutch Mom's with my other hand and put my head on her shoulder. At the end of visiting period, I will walk out between my parents, the royal family order restored, reformed. We three Kings.

"I'm just walking you to the door," I say when they move to leave. "I'm just walking with you through the door," I giggle as a staff person opens the ward door for them.

"Jade!" Authority cuts sharp in the nurse's voice.

Spoken like that, my name is a threat. Shaken, I fall back and let my parents depart.

HISTORY AND PROGRESS SHEET

History should include: Chief Complaint, History of Present Illness, Past History, Family History, Physical Examination, Tentative Diagnosis, Date and Signature.
Progress Notes should be recorded every 72 hours.

03 MARCH Much improved – had difficulty tolerating Haldol → significant postural hypotension. D/C Haldol yesterday.

Rx Continue Li^+CO_3 600 mc TID. Prn Rivotril.

May be transferred to open ward.

Ser Li^+ 1.0 mm/l.

THE OPEN WARD

On the third day I rise and follow an attendant to the Open Ward, where I am introduced to the head nurse. "Lucy . . ." I murmur, eyeing her nametag. "*Lux, luce*—that comes from the Latin meaning 'light.' That's a good name."

She starts back, then grants me a routine handshake that is the opposite of acknowledgement. "We're pleased to have you with us, Jade." We tour the ward. If I try to walk as usual, each stride ends in a flexed-ankle jerk like an arrested soccer kick. Less twitching occurs if I don't lift my feet. So, while Lucy strolls, I shuffle.

Off corridors that form three sides of a square, doors open into single, double, or quadruple rooms. Compared to PIC, the size of this ward overwhelms. Past a sprawling lounge lies the cafeteria, where people smoke at long tables. Some are privileged enough to wear their own clothes, but most are uniformed, like me, in prison-blue pajamas and bathrobes.

In the afternoon my mother finds me resting; she obtains special permission to pay me a bedside visit.

One of my classmates has asked her to deliver flowers and a letter. I skim it—anxiety about grades, the difference between an A and an A+ is minimal and shouldn't be an obsession—it's not applicable. Vaguely I register Nancy's misunderstanding and wonder how many others think I plunged into a depression. My mother and I hold hands across the blanket, and hers feels cool and solid, delicate-skinned on the back. As the afternoon sun streams in the window, it ignites the freesias on the bedside table to a luminous yellow. *Free-ja.* "Free Jade" said with flowers.

I doze as my mother reads a novel, the tassel of her bookmark dangling against her knee. In my stupor I have said little to alarm her, so she deports herself as though in a regular hospital room where a sedated patient lies recovering—from something respectable, like appendicitis.

Dad arrives after dinner, late into the visiting period. He wears an old blue suit and a tie with diagonal stripes. At my suggestion, we retreat to the empty rec room and sit on the vinyl couch to talk.

"The incest taboo is wrong because it makes people want to do it, don't you see? It's like that old saying, 'Rules were made to be broken.'"

"No. Rules weren't made to be broken, Jade." My father frowns. He crosses his right leg over his left, clasps his knee and looks straight ahead. His left leg jiggles uncontrollably, the heel half an inch off the floor.

"But in a way they are, Dad. You see the problem is

that in order for incest to be forbidden, it had to exist. But since it was forbidden, it couldn't be named—it was unspeakable. So nobody ever talks about it. We need to talk about it."

My father tucks his twitching thumb into his armpit. His eyebrows strain towards each other and his forehead pleats with worry. For a moment, anxiety clears his sight: he sees something that tortures him. The vision soon dissolves. By the glassiness of his eyes and the slackness of his jaw, I know he has absented himself.

I press on, trying to recapture his attention. "It's assumed that if two people go into a room together and shut the door, they're having sex. But they don't have to."

"Of course they don't." He leans forward and pulls himself up from the couch.

"Why are you so ashamed? The minute I bring up the topic you leave."

"It's nine o' clock, visiting hours are over," he says.

« 5 »

—Did you ever go to dances when you were younger?
—Sure. I used to play for dances!
—What?!
—I played trumpet in a band when I was in my teens. We got asked to provide the music for dances in the town hall. In the summertime we worked a lot of weddings, too. We played waltzes and fox trots, mostly, but what we really liked was swing. We jazzed it up whenever we got a chance. All the big names were touring through Calgary at that time, you know, and I used to take the bus into town. I got to hear Louis Armstrong, Count Basie, Duke Ellington . . . . Oh, it was very exciting.
—I never knew that. Why did you stop playing?
—Well, I moved away to go to university, and after that there wasn't time.
—You should have made time.
—Hm. Well, it's funny. The last dance I performed at, it was the end of the evening and we were playing God Save the Queen—in those days you had to play it at every public gathering, I think it was the law—or it was the custom, at least. Everyone would rise for it. Well, as we were playing, the other fellows in the band sat down one by one and fell silent until I was the only one left standing, blowing away on my trumpet. I was so embarrassed.

—Did you finish it off?

—Oh yes, I had the melody, so I kept going til the end. But that was it. I never played again.

« 6 »

I often used to poke in Mom's jewellery box, where rhinestone brooches flashed as though electrically lit, clip-on earrings masqueraded as pansies, and neon-orange beads hung in ropes. One day when I was seven or eight I noticed a ring that hadn't drawn my eye before and picked it up. In a tarnished gold setting was a pale, oval stone that glimmered less brightly than the rhinestones, but with the same prismatic effect. When I asked Mom about it, she looked up from changing the bed and said, "Oh. That's yours, actually."

"Mine?" I was stunned.

"Yes, it used to be your Granny's and she wanted you to have it."

"Why? Did she like me?"

Mom snapped the top sheet. "Well, she died when you were very young. She didn't know you well enough to like you."

I was pained by the thought of a grandmother who didn't like me. How well did someone have to know you in order to like you?

"So then why did she give it to me?" I clung to the idea that, secretly, she really had liked me.

"Because you were both born in October and nobody else in the family was, so you were the only one it could go to—or else it would be bad luck."

Well, that counted for something. Everyone else's

bad luck was my good fortune. "So—"

"If you want to know anything more, you'll have to ask your dad." From the tension in Mom's voice, I knew she was upset. I didn't know why, exactly, but I did know better than to ask you about that ring.

Still, after that chance discovery, I got into the habit of snooping around the house, wondering what other unexpected treasure I might find. One day I explored a corner of the basement. When I lifted a cardboard box, its bottom gave and thousands of papers spilled to the floor—an archive of clients' tax returns from the previous decade. I resealed the box and replaced it. A red Coca-Cola cooler stood next to black alligator suitcases inscribed with your initials. Another weathered case nestled beside your luggage as if it belonged there, but it was smaller and oddly shaped. I unfastened the clasp and pried open the hinges to find twisted silver tubes that belled snout-like at one end. Three keys with enamelled fingerpads. A mouthpiece. The instrument lay entombed in crushed velvet, lustreless with age.

Dad, I'm sorry your breath failed and that you packed up your trumpet.

I won't be hushed like that.

HAROLD

Harold cradled ten-month-old Jade while Harriet fried sausages. The baby's cheeks were flushed and she was bawling. She seemed in pain; Harriet planned to take her to the doctor the next day. The boys had had ear infections around her age—maybe that was the trouble. "Shhh, shhh, don't cry, sweetheart. It's all right." Harold's voice lacked conviction and, as if she could sense it, the baby redoubled her cries. Harold harboured a superstition that a constant measure of physical pain circulated in the world. If you were spared, it meant that someone else was hurting. Around a sufferer, he could not help feeling glad it wasn't him. That the one afflicted was his infant daughter salted his relief with greater guilt than usual but did not diminish it.

Being bounced on his lap usually made the baby smile and even laugh in her gurgly way. She did stop crying for a moment, but only from exhaustion. When she had caught her breath, she resumed. Still, Harold kept jogging her, trying to soothe her.

Her diapered bottom struck his groin at every

bounce. He couldn't help but get stimulated. He jiggled her faster and faster, then sprang from his chair and set her in the playpen.

Harriet looked up from the spitting sausages. The fan roared as it sucked greasy air and she had to raise her voice. "What are you doing? Can't you hold her awhile longer? Dinner's almost ready."

"Gotta go to the bathroom."

Harold rushed to the toilet and locked the door behind him. He unzipped his trousers and reached inside his shorts. He had barely taken hold of himself before ejaculate covered his hand.

Knocking on the door. "Daddy? I have to go pee." It was his three-year-old son. In the kitchen, his daughter was wailing.

JADE

At night I'm desperate to stay up and write in my Notebook. A nurse with a long nose and a mole on her chin forces me into bed. I clip my silver pen to my underwear. "Is it okay if I keep my curtains open?"

"Why would you want to do that?" When she's gone, I open them and hoist myself onto the window ledge to write by moonlight. The ledge slants into the room, though, and I start to slip off while my bed slides out. I grope for a plan and decide that if I place two chairs back to back between the bed and the wardrobe, the bed will be secure. I labour to manipulate the chairs in silence. When my pen clatters to the floor, I drop onto my belly to retrieve it and freeze until the echoes die down. I resume my efforts to move the furniture soundlessly. I must be tired because I can't avoid a few scrapes and bangs. Just as I have finally achieved my task, the same nurse flings aside the curtain of my cubicle, snorts with exasperation, and destroys my support system.

"You don't want me to put my chairs like that?"

"Why should I care how you put your chairs?" she says.

"I don't know. Why are you moving them?"

"Why do you have your curtains open? It would drive me crazy to have all those lights pouring in—whoops, I guess I shouldn't have said that, we're all supposed to be very careful about our word choice, aren't we?"

"You said I could have my curtains open."

"No wonder you're so agitated." She yanks the drapes shut.

I follow her out. "Am I allowed to go to the bathroom?"

She expels her breath. "Do you have to?"

"Yes."

"Then what do you think?"

"I don't know."

"If you have to go it makes sense that you go, doesn't it?"

"I guess so. Will it wake everyone up if I flush the toilet?"

"Is this the sort of thing you normally have a conversation about?"

"Yes. I asked my family if it bothered them if I flushed the toilet in the middle of the night and they said no."

"You've got circular logic that just goes on and on; my three-year-old can do the same thing." She moves away.

"You're the one who always answers with a question," I call after her.

"Oh, am I?"

"Yes."

"That does it, you're not the cat's meow, you know, you can't always have the last word."

She stalks off but soon returns with a needle and a strong partner. The large man grabs me and wrestles me to the bed, face down. If I scream, it will make things worse. He pinions me and leans his weight into my back. His barrel chest presses my shoulder blades. His cheek grazes mine. I smell his breath. The other nurse strips off my pants and stabs the syringe into my ass.

"Jade. Get up."

I toil to raise my lids, glimpse Harpy and her strongman at the partition. On my back, I'm plastered against the linoleum, arms stretched above my head. I arch in obedience but collapse after raising myself half an inch.

Flurry, bustle, body hoisted corpse-like onto stretcher wheeled through doors, dumped on a floor-mattress (back in PIC?)—thumbs pry open eyelids. A flashlight's narrow beam sears my pupils, panicked hands fumble me.

I flutter my lashes. "Jade, can you open your eyes for me?" a man asks.

I focus all my energy on holding up my lids. For a second I manage, then snuff out.

TIME: PATIENT PROBLEMS OR TOPIC	ASSESSMENT, ACTION, OUTCOMES (PRN'S WITH TIME IN RED)
2200	Offered medication to help her settle as speech becoming increasingly inappropriate. Refusing oral medication. Will plan on giving medication should pt be unable to settle on her own. To continue using firm, matter of fact approach w/ pt as speech gets more bizarre and argumentative during discussions. KH
2230	Haldol given I.M. KH
2300 Pt lying on floor	Pt lying on the floor responded slowly to spoken word. Pt. put to bed. BP taken 104/70. P. 120. Volume good but rhythm seems to be missing a beat at times. KH

TIME: PATIENT PROBLEMS OR TOPIC	ASSESSMENT, ACTION, OUTCOMES (PRN'S WITH TIME IN RED)
1600-2400	Parents visited & related that pt. is suspicious re: medications & possibly might try self-induced emesis after medications. Pt. later related general mistrust of parents. SD

JADE

Hours after the first forced injection, I take a piece of paper and write:

> 2 Lithium carbonate 2 X a day
> 1 Haldol 4 X a day
> 2 Rivotril 1 X a day
> 1 Cogentin 2 X a day

The struggle involved in writing nearly breaks me. I keep checking the drugs' names with the staff. My hands shake and can produce only tiny letters as quavery as the cracks on an eggshell. Reading tasks my eyes, letters swim, but to name the invading substances will help me regain some control. The drugs themselves thwart me—it's they that put tremors into my hand so I can't write, that muddle my vision so I can't read, that knock me out so I'll forget the whole process. But I keep up the fight—it's my middle name. Louise: *hear, fight*. Each act of resistance earns me another bruise. These badges soon cover my bottom in mottled shades of indigo, green and brown.

A male nurse bustles about my bed.

"Am I being moved to a single room? Am I going to have a lock on my door?" I ask, my voice a syrupy mumble.

"Yes," he says, good-natured, brisk.

In the bathroom, I lean into the mirror. My lips are chapped and flakes of skin are peeling off. I'm picking gently at the scaly pieces when a short nurse named JC barges in, grabs me by the fleshy part of my upper arm, and says, "Come on. You're going to PIC."

"No! I was only PICking the dead skin off my lip! There's nothing wrong with that."

But she's dragging me out of the bathroom, opening the communicating door between wards. As we cross the threshold, I twist and stare down at her. "Do you want to be slapped across both sides of the face?" I demand.

I tower over this flabby woman; I know I am stronger. I could hit her and hurt her like she's bruising me with her grip. Power gushes up the trunk of my body like water from roots.

"No," she says.

I let the mantle of my strength fall away. The door slams behind us.

HISTORY AND PROGRESS SHEET

History should include: Chief Complaint, History of Present Illness, Past History, Family History, Physical Examination, Tentative Diagnosis, Date and Signature.
Progress Notes should be recorded every 72 hours.

Mar 11
15⁰⁰ hrs

Did not do well on open ward.
Back in PICU.
Will follow Bili.
Repeat MSU — previously ordered but not done

Pt. is very very paranoid. Would consider schizophrenia as alternate diagnosis, time will tell.

Karl

HAROLD

"Tuck Jade into bed, Harold. I've got to do cue cards with Bruce and give Clark his nosedrops. I can't be in three places at once."

"Okay, dear. Ready for bed, Ja-dee?"

"Why isn't Mommy tucking me in?"

"Because! It's a special night."

"Why is it special?"

"Because you get to have ME tuck you in!"

"Mommy reads to me."

"Then I'll read to you."

"No, Mommy and I are reading a big kids' book together. It has chapters. We read a chapter every night. She has to read it."

"Well then I'll just give you a goodnight kiss and tuck you in. How's that?"

"I guess."

Jade crawled into bed in her nightgown. Harold edged onto the bed.

"Wow! You must be heavy! The bed bounces when you sit on it."

Harold pulled the covers up over Jade's face. "Now,

how does Mommy tuck you in? Like this?"

"No!" Jade screeched and batted the blankets out of her face.

"Like this?" Harold bent to the side of the bed and tucked the covers in between the mattress and the boxspring.

"No!" Jade kicked her legs free. "You're not very good at this."

"I'm just teasing you." He adjusted the covers and leaned over to kiss his daughter on the forehead. Unexpectedly, she twined her arms around his neck and pulled him down. She pressed her chest into his and pursed her lips. His blood stormed, his heart pounded, his innards twisted. He forgot to breathe.

At Harriet's call, he jolted upright. "Harold! Did you remember to pick up the nose drops?"

Harriet often dictated shopping lists to him over the phone while he was at work. He would stop at the drugstore on his way home and buy No More Tears shampoo.

"I'll get them for you, dear!" he called. "You get to sleep now, Jade."

Jade let go and Harold made for the door.

"You're supposed to turn off my lamp, Daddy."

Harold woke up with an erection at one a.m. He turned over. Harriet lay sprawled on her back, one arm thrown above her head. Her jaw hung loose and she snored lightly.

He slipped out of bed past the ensuite, he'd use the

other toilet not to wake Harriet, down the hall—crack of Jade's door, he looks in, enters, bed stirs when he sits. He slides down the covers quick she lies on her stomach, one pudgy cheek pressing her pillow, he yanks her nightie up over her bottom, she opens "Sshh" before she can squeal or speak "Sshh" he says nothing more. If he's silent she won't know it's him won't remember penis chafing her back doesn't give there's no channel to fill he crosses her body til flesh caves welcomes him in soft passageway in between ribcage and hip squishy yes push push yes eughhh

The whining of the hot water tap in the hall bathroom woke Harriet to the desert beside her. The pipes keened for minutes, ten, twenty? Harriet wondered what Harold could be *doing* in there, but rolled over and prepared to feign sleep.

PIC: II

In PIC, they tell me I need a bath. Two nurses, Brenda and JC, unbutton my pajamas and dunk me in a tub of lukewarm water. I jiggle while both scour me at once, Brenda at my back, JC at my breasts and belly. Then JC, the woman I declined to hit, is rubbing her gloved hand on my genitals. She stabs her sheathed finger into my vagina. The dry rubber stings and pulls. "Ow! Don't!" I yell. She jabs, tears, invades my inner passage. The walls of my vagina are starred with hot pulses of hurt. "I just want to clean your lady parts," she says, as she thrusts her finger in and out of me. She leans over me, her fat face marbled with broken blood vessels. Beneath salt and pepper bangs, her eyes pierce me.

"Now, we've got to wash your hair," Brenda says.

"No, no, let me out!"

"All right, we'll do it another way," she says. "You can kneel on the floor." I grab the enamel edge of the tub as Brenda raises high a pitcher of water and dumps it on my head. JC stands by, watching.

"No!" I cry. Brenda refills the jug and douses me.

Ropes of wet hair hang in my face and suffocate me. *Drowning. Air.* The nurse works shampoo into a lather, driving suds into my eyes and mouth. She empties several more jugfuls onto me before at last the torrent stops. "Now, how do you do your hair, in a turban?"

"Fine," I say, half-bent, trying to cover myself with my arms. JC stifles a grin and leaves without shutting the door behind her. Brenda winds my hair in a towel, weighting my head and disturbing my balance. She starts to rub my body with another towel until I insist that I can dry and dress myself. When I'm done, I shuffle into the day room in terry cloth slippers, stiff with fear of being touched.

TIME: PATIENT PROBLEMS OR TOPIC	ASSESSMENT, ACTION, OUTCOMES (PRN'S WITH TIME IN RED)
1925	Routine meds of Haldol and Cogentin given I.M. as Jade refused all meds at 1900 due to suspicious behaviour. BR
2100	Total tub bath and shampoo given. Pt. resisted same w/ inappropriate responses. Continues suspicions and mistrusting. BR

HISTORY AND PROGRESS SHEET

History should include: Chief Complaint, History of Present Illness, Past History, Family History, Physical Examination, Tentative Diagnosis, Date and Signature.
Progress Notes should be recorded every 72 hours.

14 MARCH Persistence of florid paranoid persecutory and grandiose delusions with labile moods and disinhibition. We must remind ourselves that there is always a lag time of at least 5 days before a therapeutic trial of antipsychotic medication is effective — Haldol 5 mg QID initiated 10 MARCH. There is also a significant lag time of at least one week before Lithium Carbonate at therapeutic levels is effective.

N.B. { In addition, being floridly psychotic does not equal schizophrenia !!! This lady is manic by inclusion diagnostic criteria !!!

Continue Li^+CO_3 + Haloperidol + Cogentin.
Maintain in P.I.C. for time being.

Signature

HAROLD

Harold's nocturnal risings assumed their own rhythm. Some weeks his sleep was unbroken. Other weeks he jolted awake at one a.m. several nights in a row. Each time he made for the bathroom and did indeed reach it. He wouldn't have been lying if Harriet ever asked him, "Where were you?"

But the crack of Jade's door insists; he can't help it.

Adrenaline thrills his veins, his pulse races. Just once more—each time is his last—he will follow the panicked gut-urge, he will hurry before conscience prevents him, before somebody catches him, before his girl outgrows oblivion.

He never knew how long he stood at the sink, cupping warm water and splashing his crotch. His eyes and mind glazed. The taps' whining did not wake Jade's brothers, who dreamt of dolphins trapped underwater in tuna nets, squealing.

JADE

The navy blue trench coat man, a tired old figure with his shoulders hunched, trudges down the hall as if on a treadmill, walking and walking, getting nowhere. I expect to see a string of identical cardboard cutouts circling on a conveyor belt. But instead, the trench coat approaches me, fleshes out, and I recognize it as my father. I run at him and jump, wanting him to pick me up, but he says, "Oof," and staggers.

"What's the matter? Are you that weak?"

"I didn't know you were going to jump on me!"

The cool night air clings to his dark coat. "You flew in and landed on the roof, didn't you? Is it very windy?"

"No, Jade," he says wearily.

He sits down on one of the sagging sofas which caves in so that his legs must grow longer to compensate. He fidgets with his thumb, and I wonder if he will pull the skin right off like a rubber glove.

"I can't breathe in here, the air is too dry," I complain.

I ask after Mom. Then I just contemplate his stretchy skin, wondering if it's a disguise and there's another of him underneath.

HAROLD

To any routine, one's system became inured. Harold could no longer climax from grinding into his daughter's back. The hollow between her ribcage and hip did not seem as soft anymore. He flipped her over and nosed his penis between the relaxed jaws of sleep. Her mouth enveloped him so tightly he could hardly thrust. When he ejaculated, his gasps almost masked the sound of choking.

When Jade developed chronic sore throats, the pediatrician recommended that her tonsils be removed. Harriet had qualms, having suffered a botched tonsillectomy herself, but Harold favoured the operation. Since hospitals made him uneasy, he waited until after her discharge to comfort his six-year-old.

Then he stopped at Dairy Queen on his way home from work and brought her a dish of soft ice cream every evening for a week.

JADE

Another young woman begins stalking like a bird and I join her with enthusiasm. We open all the doors so that they protrude into the hallway at right angles, then dart around them. Up, up (on our toes, wings raised), down, down (crouched, wings tucked).

The open doors will mask our escape. Up and down the hallway we fly, pausing at the lounge. "Shelley was an ineffectual angel beating his luminous wings in vain!" I cry, flapping the wings of my housecoat. My friend's eyes shine as she nods. Backing up for a good take-off, I run down the hallway, curve into my room, and take a flying leap at the window screen. For a split-second I fuse with a seagull and careen into the air—"Eee, eee." Then with a dull thud, my legs hit the ground. I open my eyes and sink back into my body.

ROYAL JUBILEE HOSPITAL
Victoria B.C.

24 HOUR PATIENT RECORD

Items to Chart	0001 — 0800	0800 — 1600	1600 — 0001
Dr's Visits		Dr. Burns	
Diagnostic Tests			None
Activity	Slept	see below	Up and about
Attitudes & Feelings	N/A	see below	See charting
Ate: eg.Well, Fair, Poor	nil	fair only	Poor. Some fluids with persuasion
Hygiene	Deferred	sponge bath	Fair - Needs assistance
Safety eg. Siderails ↑↑ or ↑↓	PIC	PIC routine	PIC routine
B.M.	∅	none reported	No problems reported
Visitors	No D. Stevens	mother E. Cooper	Parents BF?

TIME: PATIENT PROBLEMS OR TOPIC	ASSESSMENT, ACTION, OUTCOMES (PRN'S WITH TIME IN RED)
1900 Extremely determined	to elope through locked doors. Quick, agile, furtive - dashes for any door open, even a crack. SE
∞ Some deterioration noted	today in spontaneity and appropriate affect. Following a nap, some inappropriate posturing and gestures.
Possible shuffling	gait, but difficult to assess at this time, as she has just awoken. SE

DATE: Mar 15

HAROLD

Jade grew bigger and gained strength. When Harold tried to flip her, she stiffened and gripped the bed. His fingers dug deeper into her ribs to combat her resistance. She flexed round buttock cheeks, her whole body sleek with new muscles.

One night Harold opened a drawer in the ensuite bathroom. Cartoon babies crawled around the Vaseline jar, diapered bottoms raised innocently. The drawer, unpainted inside, smelt of cedar. Harold shut it and doubled back to recline open-eyed. The bedroom furniture loomed. At dawn, it glowed.

Harold's insomnia persisted for a week. Finally he rose at 1 a.m. and seized the Vaseline. The crack of Jade's door lured him in for the last time, last crime on his daughter's body—it won't show, no one will know, is she whimpering? "Sshh" it's her fault for not turning over, he greases her anus then   this time he's gone too far, really too far, a fingernail bit to the quick and then torn from the skin, orgy of horror o! open wound don't leave a mark, she's a virgin, her hymen intact, undefiled he shoves her head into the pillow to smother her screams.

•

Harriet dreamt the cat was clawing the cage of an emerald-green cockatoo. Harold was scratching himself. His fingernails, split with fungal disease, caught on his pubic hair. One hand roved his crotch all night.

From now on, this hand would never sleep.

•

Harold belonged to a birdwatching club and could identify the local fowl by song or colour. Red-tailed osprey. Great blue heron. Purple finch. Ruby tit. He watched for them in the yard while he gardened. He and Harriet planted begonias, geraniums, roses. They pruned and weeded and salted the backs of slugs to make them shrivel up.

Harold especially cared for the group of fruit-bearing trees he called his "orchard": cherry, peach, and plum. Most prized of all were the hazelnuts that bordered the neighbour's property: saplings with fuzzy bark, graceful as fawns. Harold nurtured these delicate trees from which he coaxed a tiny harvest each year. One autumn day after it had rained Harold crossed the muddy lawn. He yanked up his pantlegs to keep the cuffs dry and took exaggerated steps as if wading. He arrived to find the hazelnuts destroyed. All the limbs had been snapped off in what appeared an unspeakable rage. Sap bled from the trunks; branches lay like broken antlers on the ground.

Harold wept.

JADE

At bedtime I beg for a night light and to have my door left ajar, but they lock me into a dark cell. A crack of light seeps in and draws me to it. I poke my nose into the place where the door meets the frame and a yellow shaft opens in front of me.

Bottomless. I could step into this golden tunnel and fall, fall, into God's arms. The yellow light pulses, mesmerizes. The afterlife urges me to step past death.

I bellow as loud as I can: "Harriet, are you anywhere in this hospital?"

My mother screams back, "Yes!" clutching a door frame in resistance as they drag her off to the maternity ward to induce labour. Our cries echo from one end of the hospital to the other.

I stand on the edge of the iron bedstead and throw my weight on the door, sure it will open. The bed starts to slide, so I get down, take off my pajama bottoms and dip them in a cup of water. I rub the wet cloth underneath the bed's back legs.

Again I climb into position and drive myself into the door, leading with the top of my head, my body a diagonal vector. The bed stays in place. "I've got some exciting news for you, Mom and Dad," I shout. "We leave the womb naked!"

When I attempt to stand without support, my legs shake so violently that the mattress bounces up and down half a foot.

But, struggling to keep my balance, I throw both arms into the gymnast's 'V.' "V is for victory!" I cry. I drop to the bed and dangle my legs off the edge. My Dad appears beside me. He puts his hand on my knee. "Do you want to stay in here all day?"

"No."

"Well I just slipped in to tell you that you could come out now."

He vanishes through the keyhole. Just then, my door is unlocked and opened by a small, squeaky-voiced nurse. "You can come to the dayroom now, it's 6 a.m."

Brain fog clears as I squat on the toilet and notice the squishing of my thighs against the cool plastic seat, the sloping line of my toes against cream and beige floor tiles. Despite a full bladder, I can't urinate. Purple half-moons spangle my abdomen where I've pumped with my fingertips these past weeks to release the flow.

I ask for fresh pajamas. I brush my teeth, comb my hair and make my bed. When Dr. Burns drops by after breakfast, I show him the exemplary cell. "Everything seems to be in order here," I say to force the point.

"But I wouldn't say your behaviour has been too rational lately, would you? Flying into doors and things?"

"No, I guess not. We were just playing around."
"You'd better cool it."
"I have."

He nods his head, and we pace the corridor to the dayroom.

"How are you doing with the shakes?" I hold up my hands and strive to still the trembling, wanting to pass every test he sets me. "Not too bad," he says. "Do you know how long you've been in here now?"

"About three weeks," I say, clasping my hands behind my back. I try to mirror this man with his clean white coat, clipped phrases and cold, pale irises.

"That's just about right," he nods.

"So, when do you think I'll be able to leave?"

"We won't be too hasty. Another day in here would be best, then if all goes well we'll move you to the Open Ward."

The door of the laundry elevator is drawn back. Inside, Brenda sorts pajamas, housecoats and linen.

"Can I help you with anything?"
"You can help me fold if you like."
"I'll start with the pillowcases."

I enjoy the simplicity of this task. When I was five, my mother, after she finished ironing my father's shirts, would lower the board as far as it would go and let me press the pillowslips.

"Somebody sure won't be here much longer," Brenda says.

•

On the first day of spring, they give me back my clothes and I hang them over a chair. My jeans have shrunk in a hot dryer. My leather coat lies in folds like a shed skin—*purple, the colour of passion: Christ's suffering. Sexual pleasure.* I need to be *inviolate*. I hesitate to change, but this is the only outfit available. As I squeeze into the jeans, the denim gives a little. Though they're tight, I can zip them up. I shrug into the coat. Cool and stiff at first, it warms with wear and moulds to my shape. When I'm ready to leave, I look for my shoes. Not finding them, I ask a nurse.

"Your parents will have to bring you a pair. You were barefoot when you arrived."

DISCHARGE SUMMARY

GVHS
ROYAL JUBILEE HOSPITAL
Dr. C.J. Burns

KING: Jade
3A EMP 628343

cc. Dr. P. Montgomery

DATE OF ADMISSION: 29 February
DATE OF DISCHARGE: 21 March

This represented the first psychiatric contact and hospitalization for this 21 year old single, female University of Victoria honors, English, straight A student. She has no previous history of any psychiatric disorder whatsoever and there is no significant family history of psychiatric illness.

It is important to note that she has no history of significant drug or alcohol abuse.

As mentioned, this young female had been functioning extremely well for most of her lifetime. She had been doing well until approximately 2-3 weeks prior to admission. She became increasingly anxious and fearful and her moods became more labile ranging from euphoria to extreme fear. She, for one week prior to admission, was harboring a variety of grandiose religious delusions and persecutory delusions. She felt she had the powers to save the world, etc.

At the same time her activity level increased and she was extremely hyperactive. Her sleep deteriorated and she was experiencing virtually total insomnia for one week. She was not eating and lost some weight. Her speech became pressured with flight of ideas and her behaviour became increasingly disinhibited and she uncharacteristically became sexually provocative, at one point she disrobed in public just prior to admission.

She was brought to the Emergency Room by the police and admitted for psychiatric assessment and treatment as an involuntary patient without any insight whatsoever.

I had mentioned that there was no family history, however her paternal grandmother did experience some depressions.

Her course in hospital was not out of the ordinary. She was clearly manic, psychotic, inclusion diagnostic criteria. There was no other diagnosis that one could entertain.

It is important to note that she in no way deserves a diagnosis of schizophrenia.

By March 16 she was much improved and did not manifest any psychotic symptoms from that point onward. At discharge she was seen with her parents, incidentally her parents were interviewed on a weekly basis during her admission and have a clear idea of her illness.

Mr. King is a notary public locally.

At the time of discharge, Ms. King was not manifesting any abnormal mental symptoms whatsoever. She exhibited excellent insight, her sensorium was clear, judgement was normal.

<u>DIAGNOSIS</u>: Major-affective disorder, bipolar manic, psychotic in remission.

This is a pure biological illness.

RECOMMENDATIONS:

1. To be maintained on Lithium Carbonate capsules 300 mg AM and 600 mg HS.

She will be maintained on Lithium Carbonate for a minimum of one year. If she should experience a second manic episode within the future, life-long Lithium Carbonate maintenance therapy should be considered.

2. For the time being she will be maintained on antipsychotic medications, specifically Haldol 4 mg HS.

3. She should be maintained on Kemadrin 5 mg t.i.d. for the time being.

4. The prognosis for this girl is excellent. She should function without any significant problems as long as she is maintained on Lithium Carbonate.

Dr. C.J. Burns

TIME: PATIENT PROBLEMS OR TOPIC	ASSESSMENT, ACTION, OUTCOMES (PRN'S WITH TIME IN RED)

24-HOUR PATIENT RECORD — DISCHARGE INFORMATION

005 - A - 002 (Rev. 3/85)

DISCHARGE TIME _1500_ DISCHARGED TO _Home_ ☐ EXPIRED

DISCHARGED WITH WHOM AND HOW _Father_

REFERRALS MADE:
- ☐ HOME CARE
- ☐ DIETARY
- ☐ HOSPICE PROGRAMME
- ☐ GERIATRIC DAY HOSPITAL
- ☐ PHARMACY
- ☐ CANCER CLINIC
- ☐ DIABETIC CLINIC
- ☐ SOCIAL SERVICE
- ☐ PHYSIOTHERAPY

OTHER _____

INSTRUCTIONS GIVEN RE: _____

PRESCRIPTION GIVEN ☑ YES ☐ NO ☐ N/A   INSTRUCTION SHEET GIVEN ☐ YES ☐ NO ☐ N/A

SIGNATURE OF NURSE _J. Black_   DATE: _March 21_

« 7 »

—Do you remember, one time you asked your Mom if you could have a snack and she said no because she didn't want you to spoil your supper? You didn't argue, you just disappeared and when we called you for dinner you didn't answer. I had to go out looking for you. I found you in the field picking blackberries. You were nothing if not resourceful. You asked me not to tell your Mom on you, but you'd gotten your fingers all stained with purple juice. The thorns'd scratched you up pretty bad, you were bleeding a little bit. So we had to get you cleaned up. There was no keeping it secret.

JADE

In the ten days that follow my release, I gradually quit the drugs. With Dr. Burns on vacation, I am able to defer my next appointment until April 28th. Flanked by my parents, I visit him in the chrome and leather elegance of his private office. Chairs are grouped around a coffee table to create an illusion of casualness. I report that I've been off all medication for nearly four weeks. He asks about my final grades and I say, "Three A+'s and two A's." He rounds his eyes, impressed. "So what's your professional opinion?" I ask lightly.

"That you're going to get into trouble again." His words slam into me. "There's an eighty-twenty chance of a relapse."

I leap to my feet and he jumps after me, arms spread wide. But I only hold my head, look out the window, and say, "Jesus."

"Jade," Dad spits my name to scold me for swearing, so I add, "Please help me now." Tears pour down my face; I yank some Kleenex out of a box on the coffee table. Dr. Burns writes out a prescription and hands it to me.

"I would advise you to follow this."

"I'm glad I'm not you."

"You should know that your name is on file with the police, so that they have automatic authority to pick you up. I would advise you to fill that prescription."

"Thank you. And I'm glad I'm not you." I wipe my eyes and nose and slide back into my seat. "Before I leave, there's a few things I'd like to clear up. Remember that bump I got on my head, and my broken tooth? You told my parents I only fell. You lied. You lied by omission. I had seizures! Why did you lie?"

He smirks. "Well, yes, you did have *petit mal* seizures, but how can you remember that? If you were really having seizures, it should be a total blank for you."

A total blank: mental health. But experience isn't just erased. It lingers until sense can be made of it.

"Any other questions?"

"What about the night they overdosed me on tranquillizers, found me in a death-sprawl on the floor beside my bed, barked at me to get up, had to rush me on a stretcher to an observation room, stare into my eyes with a pinprick flashlight? All because I wanted to sit up for a while and write, like you told me I could."

"I don't have your file memorized; I have a lot of patients. I can't possibly remember what happened to you every night."

File's sitting right in front of him, but he doesn't want to be shown up by my vindictive memory again. "You said I could write by my bedside light as long as I wasn't disturbing the other patients." He widens jelly eyes flat with lack of insight and shakes his head.

Once home from the psychiatrist's office I change and head for the car. When Mom asks where I'm going I say I have to go think. "Are you going to take your medication?"

"I'm going to go think."

I drive to the Shelbourne Street liquor store, buy a cheap 750 ml bottle of white wine, find a hollow in the tall grass at Mt. Tolmie and drink half of it. I have dressed in my tight Levi's and a peach tank top, cropped to expose my midriff, armholes cut daringly wide. I've lined my eyes in sapphire blue.

It's approaching one o'clock as I arrive, breathless, at Duncan's office. I sink into the armchair.

"What did you do, run up?"

I absorb the fact of his presence. "You're here," I say. "I knew if you were here I'd be OK." Then my face contracts and sobs start. Duncan jumps to close the door. "What's wrong, Jade?"

"I saw my psychiatrist today. He wants me to go back on my medication, and I don't want to. I don't want to," I say, drawing out the repetition into a staccato of sobs.

"Why does he think that?"

"Because I was crying."

"Crying is normal, my daughter cried this morning."

"Can we go? Outside?"

Duncan swivels his chair, turning his profile to me and his gaze towards the clock on his filing cabinet. "I don't have time—I've got to go hear a thesis defense. People are counting on me."

"Yeah, that's not the point, to hurt other people." I had muddily imagined that consummation now would save me, that it was called for in this crisis.

I leave the office. The short conversation has given me no relief. I want to say: I'll make you think twice before getting implicated in the precious lifeblood of someone else. I want to throw a brick through your bedroom window. I want to rip up your lawn with the wheels of my car and smash into your flashy convertible. I want to phone your wife and embroider a true story into the pit of her stomach. I hate you for using me to test your commitment to her. I hate you for turning me on and not following through. I hate you for rejecting me to fulfill your own ends, for ignoring my need. I hate you for accepting my confidences without confiding in me yourself. I hate you for not being my lover. I hate you because I loved you and you didn't feel the same. I hate you because you're in my blood and I can't get rid of you without spilling it.

I hate you because you denigrate and downplay my experience. I hate you because you're in my way. I hate you because you're there.

I hate you because I can't have you and I hate myself for feeling that way. Why do I want what you can't/refuse to give?

How would your daughter feel about this? How would I feel if I found out my father had an affair when I was six? The rusty white and red swing set in the backyard of my childhood home. I'd play on it while he gardened. I'd shimmy up the pole while he weeded. I was addicted to the sunburst between my legs, the hot rush,

I preferred to do it when no one was around but if he wasn't too close I'd do it. How did I know how? It was my secret.

How would your wife feel about this, how much does she know? My dun-haired, aged-faced rival, yes I saw you together. She's too old for you, not what I pictured at all. How would she like it if she knew you were a cunt-tease to undergraduates? Beautiful, slim blondes who will stay perpetually young while every September, she grows another year older. The triangle will reappear. She maybe won this time but she won't win forever.

I force myself to attend Contemporary American Poetry. Class always begins with a recitation, and I volunteer to read Sylvia Plath's "Lady Lazarus": *Out of the ash/ I rise with my red hair/ And I eat men like air*. Heads turn at my delivery, and afterwards a couple of people ask if I'm all right. As I reassure them, I form a plan. Quoting Plath to Duncan won't work; he's a Renaissance man. It's not Lady Lazarus who will chill him but . . . .

Almost three o'clock. Soon Duncan will leave campus to pick up his daughter from school, and I know he will pass by his office on the way out. I approach his door, knock softly—no answer—and try the handle. Unlocked. That means he's close by. I slip inside, scan the shelves, find the book I want, and retreat behind the door. I ride adrenaline, a bucking horse that threatens to throw me. With my thumb, I mark my place in the book then clamp it shut to steady my hands. The book's edges grow damp as I wait.

The door swings open. Once he's inside I step forward, push it closed and speak as Lady MacBeth:

> The raven himself is hoarse
> That croaks the fatal entrance of Duncan
> Under my battlements. Come, you spirits
> That tend on mortal thoughts, unsex me here
> And fill me from the crown to the toe top-full
> Of direst cruelty.

Briefly, I glance up. As hoped, my audience stands transfixed, blanched, even trembling a little. My voice gains intensity.

> Make thick my blood;
> Stop up the access and passage to remorse,
> That no compunctious visitings of nature
> Shake my fell purpose, nor keep peace between
> The effect and it. Come to my woman's breasts
> And take my milk for gall, you murdering ministers,
> Wherever, in your sightless substances,
> You wait on nature's mischief. Come, thick night,
> And pall thee in the *dunnest* smoke of hell,
> That my keen knife see not the wound it makes,
> Nor heaven peep through the blanket of the dark
> To cry, 'Hold, hold!'

I toss the paperback onto his desk and he watches it land. An imposing female figure faces up. I have voiced her hatred. Evoked a bloody King Duncan, murdered in his bed. The sight of my professor at a loss for words rewards me.

Lady MacBeth claims she would have killed Duncan herself *Had he not resembled/ My father as he slept*. She balks at patricide, not regicide. But they are one for Sophocles: on the road to Thebes, Oedipus kills a man later revealed as both the King *and* his father. Father, King, Duncan. Does Duncan resemble my father? And if he did, would this quell my rage—or whet it?

At home, the Kings hound me to take my pills and my yells bounce off the white walls. I run out and want to hop in the car, but it's not mine and I know they would seize the chance to send in the cops again. So I grab my bike and pedal until my calves burn. At Cattle Point, I crouch behind broom bushes, scared that one of the passing cars will be an ambulance, or cops . . . . I listen to the surf smash on the rocks. The beating of the wind draws out my sobs. My family. They betrayed me, they turned me in to be drugged and raped. JC, Duncan, my parents—all against me. I've got no one. Wind whips the bay into choppy silver peaks. Seagulls glide and screech.

Hot tears trickle from my eyes to be blasted icy against my cheeks. The cold sea beckons to me, urges me in. I could lose myself, lose this pain-filled body, merge with the waves. There's no other way out. My mother awaits my return in the white kitchen by the red phone.

I plant my feet on the stones and clench my fists.

Below me the ocean rages, roils. I call on that power, ask it to lend itself to me. It surges up through the rocks, up through my legs. It fills the trunk of my body. I breathe deeply. I blow some of my hurt into the gale and it swirls away. I keep breathing til wind circulates through my veins. The tension in my neck and shoulders eases, and I feel a little lighter. There is one thing I can do.

HAROLD

When Harold received news that his mother had died, the opal ring was still nestled in his dress suit pocket. Six months had passed since Jade's birth; he had been waiting for the right time to show the ring to Harriet. Now it was unthinkable. It would be two more years before Harriet, taking clothes to be dry-cleaned, found it and made him explain.

Harold didn't attend his mother's funeral, although his absence dismayed the family. Still, how could he mourn what had never been? He had never enjoyed her approval. The closest she'd come to an expression of love was the day she gave him the heirloom. But it wasn't intended for him; it passed *through* him, from grandmother to granddaughter, woman to girl. Hadn't she said, "I always wanted a daughter"? He'd disappointed her in everything. If he were to grieve, it would be for a whole life spent as a motherless son.

JADE

As I leave my parents' house, bricks tumble from my shoulders into the street. Relief. I have found a room to rent in a shared house. I apply at a popular tearoom where the all-female staff wear frilly aprons in the style of Victorian maids—mostly for the benefit of American tourists, although the restaurant has a strong clientele of British expatriates. Hired as a busgirl, I'm mistaken for seventeen or eighteen by the rest of the staff, and I enjoy being incognito. Nobody asks me what I'm planning to do with my B.A.

Busgirls are almost invisible, clearing the tables like good fairies and turning them out for the next influx of customers. Nurses from the Eric Martin come in for lunch and don't notice me, even when I stare.

Sleeping in a new bed, I develop an ache in between my right hip and my ribcage. Every morning it settles in like the smell of the sea. The ache brings to mind a root of my name: *ijada, pain in the side—because jade was thought to cure this.* After it persists for several weeks, I make an appointment with a chiropractor.

"You have a strained sacroiliac joint," he announces after he has examined me and taken x-rays. "I'm just going to stretch out your back before making some adjustments." He instructs me to lie face down on the table. I feel exposed in skimpy underwear and a flimsy gown that doesn't close at the back-—I didn't know I'd have to take off my clothes. Even my bra, for the X-rays. A heavy fog of sadness fills me. Desolation out of nowhere. My face smushed against the headrest. The chiropractor stretches the spasmed area of my lower back, pushing down the elastic waist of my underpants an inch or two. Air bubbles rise from the bottom of a pool, they're going to surface and burst—*no. Stop.*

Flashes, snapshots, one: bum stripped bare; two: fingers spreading wet goop in my crack; three: weight denting mattress—a sea anemone squeezes shut. I'm shaken, shuddering to be alone in this office with this unnerving, white-coated man. But I lie still as he manipulates my body, using his weight, the strength of his hands, to make harsh snapping movements with my bones. Finally he's done. I can get dressed and go home to look up the word:

> sacroiliac: *sacrum + ilia*
> sacred + flanks, groin
> sacred + jade

That night one of my roommates, who is training to be a counsellor, tells me about her work with survivors of sexual abuse. I grip the arms of my chair as my stomach seizes up.

I am back in my childhood bedroom. The door

opens and a large purple shape with a squarish head and sloping shoulders is silhouetted against the yellow glow of the hall light. I turn towards the wall and pull the covers tighter around me. The slippered heels of the shape drag on the floor as it approaches.

It sits on the edge of my bed—the springs bounce and my whole body shifts. It rolls me onto my stomach, pinning my arms underneath my body. It leans its dark weight over me. The blankets move . . . .

A hand on my knee startles me and I twitch. "Are you okay?" Deanna asks.

"I think . . . what you're talking about—oh, there's no way! But yeah, I think maybe I . . . ."

"You've survived, that's the important part."

Assembly in Grade Two. Just before I rose from the low wooden bench to recite the Lord's Prayer, I noticed something was missing: pain. To be free of it was so remarkable that I improvised under my breath. "Give thanks for this moment. You are very lucky. Nothing hurts right now. Always remember this."

At age seven I endured spasms in my bowels and intestines that made my forehead bead with sweat. The only word I knew for the pain was "tummyache." The only remedy my mother suggested was to lie face-down on my bed.

Deanna takes hold of my hand. "You're right here. Just breathe."

I sleep on my side, back to the door. Talons dig into my shoulder blades, jolt me awake. I'm paralyzed, can't turn my head to see who's behind me. Slowly, my muscles unfreeze. I want to go to the washroom but the light switch is at the far end of the hall. I roll onto my back and stare at the ceiling, panicky, scared of the dark and who might be in it. Waiting for morning.

The next day Deanna brings home a stack of pamphlets, resources for survivors of sexual abuse: sliding-scale therapists, support groups, self-help books, crisis lines.

After my experience in the psych ward, I have no faith in the so-called mental health professions. Deanna says, "Hey, there's no pressure, you seem to be coping fine, I just thought you might want to be aware of these things."

I thank her grudgingly. As soon as she leaves the room I shove the papers under my bed.

Weeks pass. Between shifts at the restaurant, I shut myself in my room and drown in memory. A three-year-old riding my tricycle in a green and pink pinafore, my sun hat tied under my chin, white Mary Janes on the pedals. The radio muffles the sound of my bawling. Flattened on my bed, I weep until dehydration sets in. The first time I was intimate with a boyfriend I wept like this, murmuring, "I'm sorry, Daddy, please forgive me, I'm so sorry, I didn't mean to, I didn't mean to let you down, I'm so sorry, I wanted to do what you said, oh Daddy, I'm sorry I've disappointed you—you didn't want me to do this—you didn't want me to do this with anyone—do this with anyone—" ELSE boomed a voice deep within. Never do this with anyone ELSE. It winded me. ELSE changed the sentence. I knew what it meant but as a teenager living in my father's house there was nothing I could do with that knowledge except let it submerge itself again.

I slam my ticking clock in a drawer. I unplug the phone. I bite the insides of my cheeks. I can't bear the thought of grocery shopping though I'm out of food.

Grubby hands grope my breasts, my genitals, my buttocks—their imprints will never leave my flesh. I'll never be free. Could hang myself from the overhead light with a stocking, but I'm stuck to the mattress. Clothes litter the floor where I've stepped out of them, dirty dishes are stacked by the door, papers smother my desk. Grey light casts a pall on the clutter. I produced this mess and it reflects me.

I clutch my vulva, trying to protect it from the hands. It doesn't work—the handprints are inside the skin—I can't bear it. I grab a pencil and scribble on the nearest paper. My fist moves in tight circles, gouging a black knot into the sheet. The harder I press, the more pain gushes from the pencil tip. The paper rips and I chuck the pencil to the floor. I want to cut myself. I turn my wrists to study the thin greenish-blue and purple veins. The insides of my wrists look so tender, so baby's skin soft, that I let go of my fury. I rock back and forth, hugging my pillow. The light wanes.

My father is chasing me around the house with his

shirt off. Everywhere I go, he turns up. I keep running until finally he corners me. I turn and face him. "Get away from me! You RAPED me!"

He says, "You came to me, you had bare shoulders, what did you expect?"

"That doesn't make it okay."

I shake out of sleep in shock: I expected denial, not justification.

I roll onto my side and face my room. The stacked plates and cast-off clothes infuriate me. I pull on some jeans, collect the dishes and head for the kitchen, busting the tunnels I've made. I refuse to cage myself any longer.

Deanna's pamphlets have gathered dust and retrieving them makes me sneeze. I leaf through them for an hour or so, skeptically, returning often to the list of therapists. Some have graduate degrees in social work, others in psychology. None practices psychiatry—which means they can't prescribe drugs and they can't lock me up. (This much is good.)

All are women. (But then so was that nurse.)

A few describe their practice as feminist. I decide to start here.

HAROLD

At the Battle of Hastings, an arrow pierced the eye of King Harold, and the Normans conquered. 1066. Was King Harold killed, or only blinded? It matters little: sightless monarchs can't rule. Consider Oedipus Rex, who plunged brooches into his eyes to escape seeing mother-wife, father-rival, sisters-daughters, on earth or under it. Though he survived to suffer, this maiming ended his reign.

Twice in his life, Harold is afflicted with detached retinas, one in each eye. The sharp objects that enter his eyes are surgeon's tools, not arrows or brooches. Instead of destroying his vision, they restore it.

As he reaches the age at which his mother died of emphysema, cataracts renew the threat of blinding. He shatters milk bottles trying to replace them in the fridge, misses the counter with plates. He resists an operation and continues to drive.

King Harold's defeat closed an epoch in the history of England. But the language flourished: Norman French bred with Anglo-Saxon, and, half-Germanic, half-Romance, mongrel English won its way into the world.

LOUISE

Mesmerized by the dance of dust motes, Louise dimly registers the sound of Harold's car starting up. She wishes she were at the window to wave, but delivering the opal ring to Harold in the kitchen exhausted her. She sips sherry from a crystal glass.

When she regains her strength, she pulls herself to her feet, steadied by her cane, and shuffles into the piano room. She wipes the keyboard cover and hunks of dust fly up. She wheezes and coughs until, face burning, eyes watering, temples pounding, she nearly suffocates. At last the dust settles and her lungs recover. She lowers herself to the bench. After a long rest, she carefully lifts the lid. The keys have cracked and yellowed like an old woman's teeth. She touches middle C and it sings.

When Louise was four, her family took in a boarder —the schoolteacher, Miss Gunderson. A skilled pianist, she accompanied the church choir. One Thursday night, her parents at an auction, Louise tagged along to choir practice with Miss Gunderson. She watched the strange energy in her fingers as they worked the piano keys. She listened to the flow of sound that poured out the top of the upright. When Miss Gunderson stopped playing, Louise dabbled her fingers on the keyboard and assorted notes jangled to life, sounding not at all like Miss Gunderson's music. "Show me how!" Louise begged. It took a few weeks of pleading but the schoolmistress finally agreed. The first thing she showed her pupil was middle C. The place to return to when you're lost.

The note stops reverberating. Her fingers stiff with age and disuse, Louise slowly picks out Bach's "Menuet in G," one of the first pieces she learned. After a bright D with her pinky, her thumb, ready on G, initiates a five-finger climb then rounds off the phrase with two stacatto notes. The next phrase opens with an even brighter E, the progression hopeful, a clear sky, an open road. At the top of the third phrase, the drop to C pierces Louise's composure. She knows her lungs will fail before the new baby girl grows up. She will never show her granddaughter middle C. Descending notes shake and twist inside her. Sobs threaten to trigger a coughing spell that—so close to the last one—she won't survive, and she channels them into the keys. She plays on because she doesn't want to die. Teardrops fall, stacatto, at the bottom of phrases. The music weeps. It takes her place; for now, it saves her. Like the newborn who only this morning discovered her lungs, Louise can breathe.

JADE

If the job consists mostly of playing, babysitters earn their pay at bedtime. My young cousin doesn't want a story, so I entertain her by showing her my opal ring. "This ring used to belong to your great-grandmother. See how the stone looks white?"

"Yeah. Like a tiny little egg."

"Watch what happens when I hold it up to the light."

"Colours!"

"All the colours of the rainbow. Then they disappear if I move it into the shadow, see? It's sort of like a flower that needs the sun to make it open up."

"More rainbows!"

"You can dream of rainbows, you can dream you're sliding down a rainbow and landing on a big pile of feather pillows, so soft and cushiony . . . ."

She entwines my neck. "I want a drink of water."

"Shelby, you have to go to sleep now."

"No! I want a drink of water!" She grins at me, eyes sparkling, cheeks flushed. I have to admire her spunk; beside it, her brother's docility almost disappoints. When I try to move, she pulls me down with surprising strength. I plant one hand on either side of her head. I'm practically lying on her, our torsos pressed close. She giggles at her victory, her sweet breath hot on my neck.

A blood rush, prickles stir my groin, warm rain.

I stand, breaking the child's hold. "Do you really want a drink of water?"

"Yes, and someping to eat!"

"Shelby, you already had a snack and brushed your teeth. I don't think you need more food right now. But I'll bring you a glass of water if you promise to go to sleep. Okay?"

She sighs. She knows the game is over. "K."

I fetch her a glass of water.

How could I, as an adult, ever do anything else?

« 8 »

—They said I didn't start talking until I was three years old.
—No sounds, nothing? Did they think you were deaf?
—Well that was what they wondered, but then I started talking. So the joke always was, I was waiting til I had something to say.

JADE

Among the therapists I interview, one says that she helps clients discover their psyche's own mechanisms for healing trauma. I like the sound of this. If mind and body creatively transform pain, we should honour their alchemy. We could value as metamorphosis what we stigmatize as illness. An altered state can form a threshold not to be dwelt in but crossed, as in a rite of passage or a purgation. Respect for the unconscious facilitates such catharsis. Those in crisis deserve support, and certain communities give it.

In the poor quarter of a southern Italian town, musicians gather in a one-room house. A woman dressed in white reclines on floor cushions, parents beside her, friends nearby, neighbours crowding the doorway, bright ribbons in hand. Jilted by her fiancé, this woman was pining quietly when she was bitten by a tarantula. Its poison constrains her to dance, and she has hired a band to play not a wedding march but the tarantella.

The violinist bows the strings slowly, ascending the scale. The woman lies still. The guitarist joins in and when they reach middle C, the woman convulses as if stung: neck tensed, heels driven into the ground, her body a bridge between two points. As the spider that possesses her names its key, she relives the attack, wrists flexed. But even as venom compels her to move, she gyrates to expel it. Both symptom and cure, this frenzied dance forms the ritual's core.

The band launches into the piece, time kept by the tambourine. Still arched, her pelvis pressed ceilingward, the dancer takes the beat. Her head whips left to right in time and her body rides a wave of sound, buoyed up, released, buoyed up, released until the force of her legs shoots her backwards, arms spread, head a metronome. A ring of supporters watches as she loops the room on her back. She crawls, a spider personified, merged with her attacker. As an arachnid unable to stand, she flips face down, propped on her fists and the balls of her feet, her forehead marking time on the floor.

She rounds the space several times. On one turn, she pauses, entranced, by the band, her heels pounding as fast as they play. The violinist bends to her vibrating body and so surrounds her with notes that he finally bows not the strings but her body itself. Trembling, one with the tempo, she transforms from spider to conduit of meter and melody. As she channels the music, it draws out the venom. The musicians guide this evolution.

She jumps up and travels with leaps and twirls. In passing, she grabs a green ribbon and, on the spot, waves it over her head, sweeps it behind her, striking the floor with her feet fifty times in ten seconds, satin flying around her. More skipping laps, ribbon streaming. She continues for a quarter of an hour before the circle she describes contracts, her poise falters, she spins frantically then, vertiginous, drops into waiting arms.

The musicians stop playing and staunch their sweat; the dancer receives a cushion and water. After ten minutes' rest, the band strikes up again. This round and endless more proceed like the first in an hours-long ceremony. The dancer can't stop until blessed by Saint Paul. When the players sink from exhaustion, she waits, impatient for their recovery, worn but bright-eyed, far from spent.

Over time, the choreographic cycles grow briefer, the dancing looser, more varied, and injected with cries. At these signs, the onlookers wink as if to say, it approaches. On her hundredth-odd tour of the room, she freezes. With a gesture, she hushes the band. The saint speaks: *I give you grace.* The dancer glides to the edge of the room and reclines.

The ensemble plays a final reprise as a test. Free of the poison that forced her to dance, the woman rests unaffected, serene. The musicians, her family, her friends and supporters fall to their knees in thanksgiving. This year, too, the cure has been worked.

Sources

Root meanings of given names are taken from *The World Book Dictionary.* Definitions and etymologies are drawn from there and from *The Oxford English Dictionary.*

Excerpts from the DSM-IV: Reprinted with permission from the *Diagnostic and Statistical Manual of Mental Disorders*, Fourth Edition. Copyright 1994 American Psychiatric Association.

The source for the tarantella ritual described on pages 163-165 is Ernesto de Martino's *La Terre du Remords* (Paris: Gallimard, 1966).

For information regarding other Anvil Press
titles please write for a free catalogue
of books, or visit our website at:
www.anvilpress.com

Anvil Press Publishers
#204A 175 East Broadway
Vancouver, B.C.
V5T 1W2
CANADA